"I have a proposition for you."

Hank McCauley grinned. "That's a surprise, darlin', especially this early in the day."

"A *business* proposition," Gwendolyn clarified. "I represent the royal family of Belegovia on this trip to the United States. Unfortunately, Prince Alexi has disappeared."

"Oh, yeah. I saw that prince on television. Looks like he could be my twin. I don't know what I can do for you, Lady Wendy. That prince is sure not hiding out on my ranch."

She took a deep breath. "No, but for all intents and purposes, he *could* be here."

"Whoa!" Hank pulled his attention away from her quality attributes. "Don't tell me you want me to pretend to be this prince until he shows up?"

"I need your assistance, Mr. McCauley, and I'm prepared to make it worth your while."

"Lady Wendy, you shouldn't ever leave an offer like that on the table to a real Texan."

* * *

Watch for Prince Alexi's story next month, in *The Prince's Texas Bride*.

Dear Reader,

Happy New Year! January is an exciting month here at Harlequin American Romance. It marks the beginning of a yearlong celebration of our 20th anniversary. Come indulge with us for twelve months of supersatisfying reads by your favorite authors and exciting newcomers, too!

Throughout 2003, we'll be bringing you some not-to-miss miniseries. This month, bestselling author Muriel Jensen inaugurates MILLIONAIRE, MONTANA, our newest in-line continuity, with *Jackpot Baby*. This exciting six-book series is set in a small Montana town whose residents win a forty-million-dollar lottery jackpot. But winning a fortune comes with a price and no one's life will ever be the same again.

Next, *Commander's Little Surprise*, the latest book in Mollie Molay's GROOMS IN UNIFORM series, is a must-read secret-baby and reunion romance with a strong hero you won't be able to resist. Victoria Chancellor premieres her new A ROYAL TWIST miniseries in which a runaway prince and his horse-wrangling look-alike switch places. Don't miss *The Prince's Cowboy Double*, the first book in this delightful duo. Finally, when a small Alaskan town desperately needs a doctor, there's only one man who can do the job, in *Under Alaskan Skies* by Carol Grace.

So come join in the celebrating and start your year off right—by reading all four Harlequin American Romance books!

Melissa Jeglinski
Associate Senior Editor
Harlequin American Romance

THE PRINCE'S COWBOY DOUBLE

Victoria Chancellor

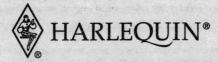

TORONTO • NEW YORK • LONDON
AMSTERDAM • PARIS • SYDNEY • HAMBURG
STOCKHOLM • ATHENS • TOKYO • MILAN • MADRID
PRAGUE • WARSAW • BUDAPEST • AUCKLAND

To my literary agent, Linda Kruger, for her consistent
support in good times and bad.
Here's to the future!

ISBN 0-373-16955-8

THE PRINCE'S COWBOY DOUBLE

Copyright © 2003 by Victoria Chancellor Huffstutler.

This edition published by arrangement with Harlequin Books S.A.

Visit us at www.eHarlequin.com

Printed in U.S.A.

ABOUT THE AUTHOR

After twenty-eight years in Texas, Victoria Chancellor has almost qualified for "naturalized Texan" status. She lives in a suburb of Dallas with her husband of thirty-one years, next door to her daughter, who is an English teacher. When not writing, she tends to her "zoo" of four cats, a ferret, five tortoises, a wide assortment of wild birds, three visiting chickens and several families of raccoons and opossums. For more information on past and future releases, please visit her Web site at www.victoriachancellor.com.

Books by Victoria Chancellor

HARLEQUIN AMERICAN ROMANCE

844—THE BACHELOR PROJECT
884—THE BEST BLIND DATE IN TEXAS
955—THE PRINCE'S COWBOY DOUBLE*

*A Royal Twist

All underlined places are fictitious.

Chapter One

Lady Gwendolyn Reed straightened her plum wool suit jacket, squared her shoulders in the best tradition of the British nobility, and watched the so-called cowboy approach the screen door from inside the darkened house. Backlit by a window at the end of the hallway, he appeared tall and broad shouldered. Instead of hurrying, as would be proper in this situation, he sauntered with a rolling gait she'd only seen previously in Western films.

A tiny bead of perspiration traveled down her back, keeping time with the cowboy's slow, steady pace. Who would have imagined early May would be so dashedly hot, even in Texas?

Gwendolyn resisted the urge to tap her foot on the wide wooden planks. She didn't want to be here. Looking back briefly to the black Land Rover parked in the gravel drive, she was at least assured she wasn't alone. A very nervous valet watched her from behind tinted glass. The driver—an Austin resident who had grown up driving on the wrong side of the motorways—appeared stoic and unaffected, as usual.

One must have nerves of steel to negotiate the frightening dual carriageways and twisting rural roads of Texas, where everyone drove large vehicles—from huge lorries to caravans on holiday—at an alarming rate of speed.

"Mr. Hank McCauley?" she asked as the man stopped before her.

"That's me, darlin'," he drawled, running a hand through his too-long hair. He opened the thin barrier of the screen door and stepped outside. Dressed in low-slung jeans, a white towel draped around his shoulders, he appeared as though he'd recently stepped out of the shower. His long bare feet told her she'd interrupted his morning—his very late morning—grooming. His stubble indicated he hadn't shaved yet today. He ran a hand through sun-streaked, tousled brown hair.

He looked just like a James Dean-ish, Hollywood-style version of Prince Alexi Ladislas of Belegovia.

Oh, my. Gwendolyn looked up into his sleepy, hooded blue eyes, telling herself that she should be evaluating this Texan for his suitability, not comparing his masculine attributes to the prince. Still, any woman would appreciate his tall, broad-shouldered form, his smooth, tanned skin, and the intangible air about him that screamed—no, make that whispered in a bedroom voice—*I am one-hundred-percent male.*

Odd that Prince Alexi, who appeared the mirror im-age—albeit a more polished one—of Hank McCauley had never affected her this way.

She blinked away the notion of cool sheets and warm showers, clutching her combination purse and briefcase tighter until she was sure she'd left imprints in the leather. "Mr. McCauley, my name is Lady Gwendolyn Reed and I have a proposition for you."

He grinned. "Well, that's a real surprise, darlin',

especially this early in the day. Most of those come at night out at Schultze's Roadhouse.''

She assumed this roadhouse was some type of pub, one this man frequented with some regularity. "A *business* proposition," Gwendolyn clarified, fighting the urge to lose her composure completely on the porch of this ranch house in the Texas Hill Country. She wondered what King Wilhelm would say if she pulled her hair loose, threw down her briefcase and ran screaming across the blue-and-red flower-dotted countryside.

She'd had a very bad morning.

"I represent the royal family of Belegovia on this trip to the United States. Unfortunately, Prince Alexi—you may have read or heard of his trip to Texas—has disappeared.''

"Oh, yeah. I saw that prince guy on the television. Looks like he could be my twin," Mr. McCauley said with a heart-stopping grin.

"Yes, well I'm sure the two of you are unrelated, although the resemblance is remarkable. Prince Alexi, of course, grew up in England while the royal family was in exile.''

"You don't say. What did they do wrong?''

"Wrong?''

"To get exiled.''

Gwendolyn gritted her teeth. "Their only crime was to be taken over by the Soviet Union after World War II. The monarchy was restored to Belegovia after the breakup of the communist government.''

"Ah, one of those political things.''

"Quite. Now, as I was saying, I need your assistance.''

He leaned against the door frame, close enough that

Gwendolyn smelled his spicy cologne and envisioned a diamond-bright sparkle coming from his sexy grin. "What can I do for you, darlin'?"

"May I come inside so we may talk?"

He straightened, using one arm to push the screen door wider. "Come right on in, Wendy."

"That's Lady Gwendolyn."

"We're not much on titles in the U.S. of A."

"So I've heard. In that case, you may call me—"

"Darlin', you look just like a Wendy to me."

She closed her eyes and counted to ten. *Be nice to the man. He's probably the only person in this barbaric land who looks exactly like Prince Alexi.* Thankfully, she'd overheard the rather vivacious waitress—the very reason Alexi was now missing—mention Hank McCauley's name and hometown.

He leaned close enough that she saw a tiny crescent-moon scar to the right of his upper lip. "Lady Wendy, you shouldn't ever leave an offer like that on the table to a real Texan."

HANK WASN'T SURE WHAT the pretty English lady's game was, but he was curious enough to listen. He hadn't planned to do much except take a nap after his shower, anyway. All-night colic sessions took a lot out of him. Fortunately, the mare he'd walked and dosed until long past dawn had finally settled down.

"Pardon the mess," he said, grabbing a denim work shirt off the arm of the couch with one hand and a cold mug of coffee with the other. "I'd tell you it was the maid's day off, but that would be a lie. She's been gone a good three months that I can recall."

He saw indulgent sympathy in her eyes. "That's

quite all right, Mr. McCauley. Perhaps my offer will lead to the hiring of new housekeeper.''

He needed another ten hours in his day, not money for a housekeeper. But he wasn't about to admit that to the lady until he learned why she was here. ''Have a seat, Lady Wendy, while I put this stuff in the kitchen. I'd offer you some coffee, but I don't have a fresh pot made.''

She perched on the edge of his momma's old colonial American sofa. He sure did love that couch. Had a few happy memories...but maybe he shouldn't think about those right now.

''Actually, I prefer tea,'' the English lady said, ''but please don't prepare any. I'd rather we got right down to business.''

''I like a lady who knows what she wants,'' Hank said from around the corner of the kitchen as he tossed the shirt onto a chair and put the mug on the counter. The smell of the hours-old coffee, which had nearly burned in the pot before the coffeemaker turned itself off, filled the air. He briefly considered putting on a shirt, but he kind of liked the way Lady Wendy tried not to stare at his chest. When he didn't have busted ribs or some big old bruise, he considered his chest and a fairly respectable six-pack of abs two of his best features.

''So what business brings you to Ranger Springs?'' he said, taking a seat in a leather recliner with heat and massage features. That chair had sure felt good on his aching joints when he was still on the circuit. At the moment, the cool leather gave him a little jolt against his bare back.

Lady Wendy was perched on the edge of the couch, that funny-looking purse lying flat on her lap. She had a death grip on the fine-grained leather. Instead of long talons or work-shortened stubs, she had natural-looking, clear-polished nails that looked real classy. "I'm employed by the royal family of Belegovia. I'm charged with coordinating the prince's tour of Texas for the purpose of expanding economic opportunities and tourism."

"I saw something about the prince on the news yesterday. He's been up in Dallas, hasn't he?"

"Yes. We had several engagements there before traveling to San Antonio."

"Is that where you're headed? 'Cause I have to tell you that you made a little detour."

Maybe he should have made her that hot tea so she'd have something to do with her hands besides holding that purse in a death grip. "I'm aware of where I am and why, Mr. McCauley."

"Why don't you call me Hank, Lady Wendy? We Texans don't stand on formality."

"Since my proposition is a business one, I'd prefer to keep our discussions less personal."

He shrugged. "Whatever you like. So, what's this proposition?"

"First, I must insist this conversation remain confidential between the two of us."

He nodded. "I'm a man of my word." As much as he'd like to brag he'd been propositioned by a classy English lady, he'd listen to her story and keep their discussion to himself.

She took a deep breath, giving him a pretty good view of her breasts. Not buckle-bunny, pop-the-snaps quantity, but nice nonetheless. "It appears the prince has decided to take his own holiday."

Hank pulled his attention away from Lady Wendy's quality, not quantity, attributes. "What?"

"Prince Alexi has taken a short deviation from our planned itinerary. I'm not sure when he'll return."

"Is this a problem?"

"It may be. You see, we have two events in San Antonio, a dinner in Austin, then we hoped to meet with the president if he is going to be at his ranch for the weekend."

"I guess you don't want to stand up the president."

"I don't want to cancel any of these events. Prince Alexi can be...difficult, but I certainly didn't expect him to leave me in the lurch."

"So, are you and this prince an item?"

"I beg your pardon!" If possible, her spine got even straighter. He could probably bounce a quarter off her deltoids.

"You know what I mean. This sounds a bit personal. Are you and the prince...involved?"

"Absolutely not! I've known Prince Alexi Ladislas since we were both public-school mates in England, and I've never considered him anything more than a friend."

"Ah, so it is personal."

"Not in *that* manner."

"But he's your friend, meaning he let you down."

Lady Wendy seemed to deflate just a bit. "I should have anticipated something like this. There was an unfortunate incident with an actress in Monaco last fall..." She seemed to shake herself away from her memories. "He's been restless lately, more so since we'd planned this trip to the States."

"I don't know what I can do for you, Lady Wendy. That prince is sure not hiding out on my ranch."

"No, but for all intents and purposes, he *could* be here."

"What do you mean by that?"

She took another deep breath, then bent forward just enough to pull that silky material tight against her breasts. "You really are the very image of Prince Alexi, Mr. McCauley. With just a proper—I mean a similar—haircut and his wardrobe, I know that we'd be well on our way to—"

"Whoa! You want me to pretend to be this prince until he shows up?"

"Exactly," she answered with more enthusiasm than he could have imagined. "With any luck, we'll be able to contact Prince Alexi within twenty-four hours. I'm sure he'll see reason and return to his entourage. Unfortunately, canceling the events until his return would appear suspicious, even if I were to come up with a good excuse."

"Why? Is he involved in something shady?"

"Shady?"

"You know…illegal, immoral or just a little crooked."

"Absolutely not! He's a fine, upstanding man from one of Europe's oldest royal families. He's educated, intelligent and heir to a kingdom."

Hank narrowed his eyes. "You sure you aren't sweet on this guy?"

"No! And besides, even if I were, that's beside the point."

"Which is…?"

"I need your assistance, Mr. McCauley, and I'm prepared to make it worth your while."

"How's that?"

"While the treasury of Belegovia does not rival

those of Great Britain or the Arab world, I can offer you a substantial fee for only a few days of your time.''

Hank shook his head. ''I've got chores to do, horses to tend. Twenty-five bags of sweet feed are bein' unloaded this afternoon. This ranch doesn't run by itself, Lady Wendy.''

''Surely you can hire someone to fill in for a few days. If we get started immediately, I can have any alterations made to the wardrobe, brief you on the itinerary and give you some lessons on protocol.''

''Protocol, hmm? In other words, you'd tell me what to do and say. Tell me, Lady Wendy, how are you gonna explain my Texas accent?''

''I would, of course, give you elocution lessons.''

''You'd teach me to speak like some foreign prince in less than a day? I don't think so.''

''Prince Alexi speaks English flawlessly. He grew up in England while his family was in exile. He even lived in the States for five years before returning to Belegovia.''

''Did he live in Texas?''

''No, Boston.''

''Then he might as well talk like you, Lady Wendy, because Texans can barely understand those fast-talking Yankees.''

''Surely with a little practice...''

Hank shook his head. ''No offense, Lady Wendy, but I don't think you've thought this plan through. Maybe it would be best to just tell everyone he's sick. Food poisoning, or a summer cold. Those can be pretty nasty.''

''I've always found the 'sudden illness' reason generates rabid speculation by the press. The tabloids might fabricate ridiculous stories that would make Prince Alexi's character seem in question. He's never taken drugs, nor does he drink to excess, but that is the first thing they would write. No, I simply cannot suddenly state that he is ill. Besides, any sickness serious enough to warrant canceling the trip would worry his family needlessly."

"You could always tell them the truth, that he's run off for a couple of days," Hank suggested gently.

"I can't do that to the king. Although I didn't grow up in Belegovia, I've grown quite fond of the country and the royal family."

"I'm just not sure I can help you. I've never really tried, but I don't think I'm much of an actor." He'd talked to one of those Hollywood types about a role in a film once while a movie company had been in Austin, but Hank just didn't see himself as a either a "pretty boy" or a thug, and he sure didn't want to play some stereotypical Texas cowboy. He sure wasn't a prince. Nope, he was a horse trainer now.

She seemed to deflate, slumping back against the sofa. The fire went out of her pretty whiskey-colored eyes. "I'd so counted on a successful trip...the triumph that would bring needed revenues into Belegovia. The country has come so far in so few years, but King Wilheim has such plans...plans Prince Alexi shares. But as of this morning, he's off with a petite blond waitress from that truck stop on the interstate, and I—"

"Kerry Lynn? He's gone and run off with Kerry Lynn Jacks?"

"I believe that is her name. As a matter of fact, she gave me the idea of asking you to fill in for the prince—indirectly, of course, since she had no idea she would be running off with the prince at the time—when she mentioned you and she were once involved.''

''Not serious. But that's beside the point. What in the world was Kerry Lynn thinkin', runnin' off with some foreign prince?''

''I believe he was being noble at the time. Something about her unreliable car and a trip to see some relatives... Besides, he can be most compelling when he applies himself.''

''But still, she's no fool. He must have fed her a line of bull.'' Hank shook his finger at the British lady as he leaned forward. ''If that prince so much as lays a finger on her, he'll be answerin' to me!''

''*She* kissed *him!*''

''What?'' He slumped back into the recliner.

''Right there in the truck stop, she kissed him. She thought he was you, and she threw her arms about his neck quite enthusiastically and kissed him on the mouth.''

Hank smiled. ''Kerry is a bit impulsive. I hadn't been by to visit in quite a while and I suppose she was just glad to see me.'' Hank rubbed his bristly chin. ''Say, what date is this, anyway?''

''Wednesday, May 8.''

''Dang it! I'll bet Kerry thought I was bringing her a graduation present. She's getting her degree from Southwest Texas State University on Saturday.''

Lady Wendy looked a bit green. ''How old is this young woman?''

''Well, she's three years younger than me, so that would make her twenty-eight.''

The lady seemed to relax. ''I thought for a moment

that Prince Alexi had run off with someone... younger.''

He almost heard her unspoken words—*much younger*. Jailbait younger. Hank had to chuckle despite the serious situation of Kerry being off on her own with some foreign prince. ''She's been going to college part-time for as long as I can remember 'cause she helps her mother and sisters by working as a waitress.''

''If she's graduating on Saturday, surely she won't be gone long. Today's Wednesday. If you'll agree to stand in for the prince, I'm sure it would only be for a day or two. Miss Jacks will return with him, you and Prince Alexi can switch places, and we'll continue the tour as planned.''

Hank shook his head again. ''Haven't you been listening? I'm a Texan, not some fancy foreigner. I can't talk like I grew up in Europe and lived in god-awful Boston for five years.''

Lady Wendy brightened. ''If that's your only objection, then we'll give you a sore throat. Laryngitis won't cause any suspicion from the press.''

''Whoa, now! I didn't say that was my only objection. I'd like to point out I don't exactly act like a prince.''

''I can teach you.''

Hank settled back against the body-warmed leather and thought about the offer. A couple of days with Lady Wendy, learning to be a prince. No doubt eating with his pinkie sticking out. He almost grimaced at the image. For all he knew, this Prince Alexi was some dandified intellectual who knew all about Beethoven and nothing about George Strait. He probably thought Garth Brooks was some little ol' stream in Wisconsin.

On the other hand, it wouldn't hurt to learn some manners. Like how to eat those tiny snacks they always served at country clubs. How to order something besides a longneck if he wanted a drink. How to wear something besides new jeans and a clean shirt when he wanted to dress up.

Rich cutting-horse owners often asked him to join them in their boxes during competitions. He also had to go to cocktail parties and some fancy dinners in Houston and Dallas—sometimes even outside of Texas—to meet the kind of people who could afford a twenty- to fifty-thousand-dollar horse. He knew he needed some polish, but so far he'd gotten by with his grin and his championship bronc-riding buckle.

If anyone could make a silk purse out of a sow's ear in just a day or two, Hank had a real good idea Lady Wendy was the person. She'd at least give it a good British try, he thought with a grin.

"You know, I could probably call Kerry's momma, Charlene Jacks, at the Four Square Café to find out where they all went," Hank said.

"But you don't quite understand, Mr. McCauley. If the prince doesn't want to be found, if he doesn't want to come back, nothing will convince him otherwise. I think our time will be best spent training you for tomorrow's events, then we can find the prince. Or perhaps he will come back. He always does."

Hank thought about this for a moment. He really didn't want to end this opportunity so quickly, even if they *could* locate the prince *and* convince him to come back. Plus he was very intrigued by the formidable Lady Wendy.

She'd looked so forlorn at the prospect of failing. He wasn't sure why this job was so important to her—

she wasn't from Belegovia, and she'd claimed she wasn't sweet on the prince—but whatever the reason, all the starch had gone out of her when he'd questioned her plan. He wasn't sure he could act like some European prince, but he couldn't live with the idea that *he'd* failed her.

"Laryngitis, hmm?" he asked, still grinning. "I'll cut my hair. I'll even wear this prince's fancy clothes. But don't think I'm gonna stick out my pinkie when I drink out of one of those sissy china cups."

GWENDOLYN SUPPRESSED A sigh of relief when Mr. McCauley acquiesced to her plan for him to impersonate the prince. At least he'd give it a good try, she was sure, because for some reason he'd decided to help her. It wasn't the money; something else motivated Hank McCauley. Perhaps he wasn't as broke or lazy as he appeared. She certainly wished she knew what did motivate him, since she would no doubt need that knowledge later, when instructions were going poorly and he threatened to walk out. Which he probably would.

Truth be told, she wasn't entirely certain she could turn this casual, flirting, unrefined cowboy into Prince Alexi in less than twenty-four hours. However, the idea of reporting her failure to King Wilhelm was unconscionable. She had to try. And Milos Anatole, Prince Alexi's valet, would help tremendously.

The idea of telling her father she'd been dismissed from her first independent job, especially one with the royal house of Belegovia, was appalling.

"Very good, then, Mr. McCauley. If you'd like to pack a small bag with any personal toiletries, we'll be off."

"Whoa, now. I have to make arrangements for someone else to help Juan take care of my stock. I can't just walk away from seventeen horses, four laying Rhode Island Reds, and the best mouser in the state of Texas."

Gwendolyn wasn't sure what he was talking about—probably some types of animals—but he sounded responsible for them. "Perhaps this Juan person can handle the task. Or surely you have a friend or a neighbor who can help."

"Well now, I have somebody I can call, but I've got to see if he's available. He's got his own place to take care of."

Gwendolyn glanced at her watch. If they got on the road within the hour, they could arrive in San Antonio before two o'clock that afternoon. That would give her nearly twenty hours—if they had to work through the night—to get Mr. McCauley ready for the children's hospital and zoo appearances tomorrow.

"Let's get on with it, then." She rose from the couch and clutched her briefcase in front of her with both hands.

Mr. McCauley frowned, leaning back in his chair to look her in the eye. "Are you always this bossy?"

She swallowed a caustic reply. "I'm sorry, Mr. McCauley, but we are on a tight deadline. If there is anything I can do to convince your friend to arrive promptly, please let me know."

"How much were you gonna pay?"

She suddenly realized they hadn't discussed a fee. "How much do you require?"

"We'll talk about me later, but why don't you pay my friend five hundred to stay here and watch my spread? That'll cover about two days of his time."

From knowing Prince Alexi—who had the uncommon ability to compute pounds to yen to euros—for so many years, she'd learned to compute foreign currency. Five hundred dollars seemed fairly reasonable. About ten dollars an hour American, if one counted the entire day and night. "Very well. I'll have a check prepared for him."

"Now, Lady Wendy, I'm not sure the bank in Ranger Springs will let him cash a check from Europe."

Gwendolyn felt her body go rigid. "I assure you—"

"Now, don't get all bent out of shape. This is a small town. Hell, a lot of people won't take a check from Oklahoma, much less Belegovia. Why don't you run into town and see if you can get some cash? I'll get dressed, pack a bag and be ready to go when you get back."

"This is absurd! A check from the royal treasury of Belegovia is absolutely valid!"

Hank McCauley shook his head, making a lock of unruly hair fall into his hooded eyes. "No cash, no deal."

Gwendolyn swallowed another reply and turned on her heel. "Very well, then, Mr. McCauley. Your friend will have his cash. I'll be back shortly. Kindly be ready to leave when I return."

"You've got it, Lady Wendy."

She heard the recliner squeak as he rose, but his bare feet made no sound on the floor. She couldn't keep herself from looking back to see where he was located.

He was right behind her. She turned and clutched her briefcase high against her chest, drawing in a deep breath, inhaling his clean fragrance and spicy cologne.

Why didn't the man at least don a shirt? He was absolutely improper.

Absolutely intoxicating, she had to admit as her head swam.

"You might want to stop by the Kash 'n' Karry on your way back from the bank. I'll need a couple of six packs of Dr. Pepper—the real kind, not that diet stuff—while we're working on this prince thing."

"Dr. Pepper." She was relieved her voice still worked. "Anything else?"

"Throw in some Doritos, will you, darlin'? I've got a good idea all this training is gonna make me hungry as well as thirsty, and I doubt they have my kind of food on the menu at the hotel where we'll be stayin'."

Hotel. The two of them, working until the wee hours, alone in a suite. Maybe not alone, if she could keep Milos with them all night. "Whatever you wish, Mr. McCauley."

He stepped even closer, so close she had to look up into his blue eyes and heart-stopping grin. Too dangerous. She dropped her gaze. She could see the sprinkling of hair on his fingers as he gripped the towel around his neck. His chest appeared warm, broad and firm underneath those fisted hands. She had the irrational and totally inappropriate urge to taste his skin.

Good heavens! What was wrong with her?

"Now, Lady Wendy, what did I tell you about not leavin' an offer like that on the table?"

"What?"

He grinned. "Never mind. You run off to the bank, now, and don't forget those Dr. Peppers."

TRAVIS AUSTIN WHITTAKER had just paid for a pound of ten-penny nails, a box of staples and two rolls of chicken wire when his cell phone rang. Getting his change from Jimmy Mack Branson at the hardware store, he unclipped the phone from his belt.

"Hello."

"Travis, I need a favor."

"What's up, Hank?"

"I need to go out of town for a couple of days, real unexpected. Can you come over and help Juan? He needs to be home with his family at night. Also, I've got a new horse coming in on Friday and I'm not sure what time I'll be back."

"Sure, I'll be glad to." He paused as he held the door open for two ladies. "Got a hot prospect on a new horse?"

Hank chuckled. "Kind of a hot prospect, you might say, but not the four-legged variety."

"Whoa. That's news."

"Well, not exactly. I need to keep this real quiet, Travis. Can you do that for me?"

"Sure, buddy. No problem. Will you have your phone with you?"

"Of course."

"Then I'll call if anything comes up I can't handle."

"Thanks. I'm paying you for this."

"No way."

Hank laughed. "Yeah, I've gotten you a great deal. I'll fill in the details later."

"Whatever." Hank knew that Travis didn't need the money. Besides, he wouldn't take payment from a friend and neighbor. "I'll come by late this afternoon if that's okay."

"Sure. Juan leaves around five o'clock usually."

"See you when you get back."

Travis hung up the phone and shook his head. So Hank was finally seeking out some female companionship. Good for him. As far as Travis knew, Hank hadn't been in a serious relationship for months. He'd sworn off women after he quit the circuit because the gossips of Ranger Springs could sure do a number on a man's reputation if he wasn't careful. Just look at what had happened to Grayson Phillips—they'd hounded the poor man into matrimony last year, not that Gray seemed to mind being married to Dr. Amy Wheatley, Travis recalled with a chuckle.

So Hank was going off with a woman for two days. Well, Travis sure hoped he had a real good, relaxing time. Nothing like a little R and R to put a smile on a man's face.

Chapter Two

He might be a rogue and a scoundrel, but he was a man of his word. He was ready to go when she returned from the bank. A well-worn carryall sat next to his chair on the porch while a large, fat yellow tabby cat wove its way through his legs.

Presumably the "best mouser in the state of Texas."

Gwendolyn stepped down from the Land Rover, motioning Prince Alexi's valet to follow her. She'd prefer to make the introductions before they all climbed back into the vehicle for the short trip to San Antonio.

"Would you care to join us, Mr. Boedecker?" she asked the driver.

"You go right ahead, Lady Gwendolyn. I'll get to know Mr. McCauley later."

Yes, at least the two men would have something in common. Same state, same economy of language. They no doubt enjoyed activities like drinking beer and flirting with women.

Well, she thought, pulling her jacket straight and marching toward the porch, Mr. McCauley would *not* be flirting with women for the next few days. Not as

Prince Alexi. She didn't want any rumors to get back to King Wilheim, who was intent on his eldest son marrying a suitable woman from European nobility as quickly as possible. Gwendolyn prayed that no word of Alexi's impulsive little trip with the truck-stop waitress reached the king's ear.

Hank McCauley rose from the wooden chair, stretching until she was certain the pearl snaps on his shirt were going to pop open. Ridiculous idea. Why in the world did these cowboy types prefer shirts without proper buttons?

"Mr. McCauley, I'd like to present His Royal Highness Prince Alexi's personal valet, Milos Anatole, who will be assisting you with clothing and personal grooming." She gave a slight nod, and Milos, who was very proud of his position as attendant to the future king of Belegovia, stepped forward and bowed.

"No offense, Mr. Anatole, but I'd just as soon get dressed on my own."

"Milos will be indispensable to you in making the correct wardrobe choice," Gwendolyn pointed out.

"He can pick 'em," McCauley drawled, "but I'm doin' up my own buttons and zippers."

She suppressed a smile, noticing that Mr. McCauley's drawl became much more pronounced when he stressed his Texas roots and independent ideas. "I'm sure we all understand your need for privacy."

He frowned at her, but she plunged ahead before he could make any further remarks. "Milos will also assist with your instruction and other details such as protocol and menu."

"You just tell me where to go, when to be there and what to wear, you hear?"

Good heavens, but Hank McCauley was laying it

on thick today! Perhaps he was trying to convince them all that he was as opposite to Prince Alexi as night and day. Well, she'd just see about that! When she was finished with him, he'd be able to stand next to the prince and confuse even close acquaintances.

She only hoped she could fool the paparazzi and the king.

"Well, let's be off then," she said cheerfully. "Mr. McCauley, I'd suggest you sit in the back where the windows are tinted darker until we work more on your princely bearing."

"Whoa again, Lady Wendy. I'm perfectly willing to go with you and help out with this impersonation, but I'm not squeezing myself into the back seat of that vehicle and taking off for San Antonio. No self-respecting cowboy would get himself stranded in town with no way back home."

"We will, of course, provide transportation when Prince Alexi returns."

"Nope. I need my own truck."

Gwendolyn resisted the urge to place her hands on her hips and stamp her foot like an irate fishwife. "Mr. McCauley, we need to start work immediately on the history of Belegovia, the itinerary and all the details that you will need to know as Prince Alexi." And she sincerely doubted she could get any work done in a rattletrap truck strewn with paper rubbish and beer cans. Not that she'd actually seen any of that debris around Mr. McCauley yet...

"Then you come with me and start working. I'm driving my own truck to San Antonio or I'm staying right here."

Stubborn man! She would have gladly strangled him if she didn't need his neck to be free of bruises for the next few days. "Very well," she said as civilly as possible under the circumstances. "Let me get my briefcase and I will begin instructions at once."

"And bring me one of those Dr. Peppers, darlin'," he called out as she turned away.

She gritted her teeth and shooed the other man back to the Land Rover. "Make a list of whatever you feel is most urgent for Mr. McCauley's education. We'll meet with him in the suite after checking in to the hotel. I trust we've already made arrangements to enter through the service elevators?"

"Of course," Milos answered. "No one except for a few maids will see the *prince* enter the hotel."

"Very good. Call me on my mobile if you think of any problems."

After retrieving a cold can of the soda, her sunglasses—a recent addition to her wardrobe caused by the unrelenting glare of the sun on the shining bonnet of the Land Rover—and her briefcase, she made her way with as much dignity as possible to the porch, where Mr. McCauley awaited. At least he was fully dressed. She should have thought to give him a selection from Prince Alexi's wardrobe, but she'd been so shaken when she left his ranch to go into town that she hadn't planned that far ahead. She sincerely hoped this was not an omen of things to come.

"Let's be off," she repeated, handing him the can.

"Yes, Your Highness."

"Really, Mr. McCauley," she said as he took her arm and steered her around the side of the house, "your sarcasm is unnecessary and inappropriate. I am the daughter of an earl, not a member of the royal family." She took a deep breath as she rushed to keep up with his longer stride. "Prince Alexi would certainly never say such a thing to an employee."

"I'm beginning to think this prince is a real bore."

"Absolutely not! He's a wonderful man."

"He sounds like a sleazy toad who just ran off with my former girlfriend."

"You claimed that you and Ms. Jacks were not that close."

"That's beside the point. I'm not real fond of this prince right now."

Gwendolyn wasn't real happy with him, either, but she wasn't about to admit that to Mr. McCauley.

They stopped beside a huge, flashy pickup truck with a ram's head emblem on the side. It was spotlessly clean, and the dark blue finish featured tiny, glistening metallic flecks that reflected the unrelenting Texas sunshine. The monstrous vehicle was so tall that it needed a step for passengers to climb inside.

Hank McCauley reached up, opened the door and gazed at the interior. "You just throw that gimmee cap in the back and boost yourself up into the dually. I'll get us to San Antonio pronto."

"I beg your pardon?"

"What?"

"Did it ever occur to you that the rest of the world speaks English, while you are communicating in some language that is incomprehensible to the average person?"

Hank McCauley threw back his head and laughed. Of all the gall! Gwendolyn was sorely tempted to kick him in the shin, just as she'd done to Prince Alexi when they were school chums in England and he'd teased her about a particularly lovely little straw hat she'd worn…just once.

"I'll tell you what," Mr. McCauley said as he grabbed her around the waist and lifted her to the steps of the monster truck. "You teach me proper English, and I'll teach you Texan."

She let out a gasp as she tottered on the step, bringing her eye to eye with the irritating cowboy.

"Easy does it, Lady Wendy." His warm hands steadied her. "First lesson. This truck is a dually because it has dual wheels on the back. That's for hauling horse trailers and other heavy equipment. Second lesson," he said, his warm blue eyes crinkling in humor, "a gimmee cap is a cap with a logo that you get free from somebody who wants to sell you something. Like John Deere or Purina. Got it?" He didn't wait for her reply. "Now you get your cute little butt inside the truck and don't touch anything. You can start lecturing me as soon as I get on the road."

With that, he turned her around—quite effortlessly, she noticed—and actually patted her on the bottom!

"Well!" she exclaimed, but she was already pulling herself onto the seat. His chuckles faded as he walked around the back of the "dually." He probably told every woman he met that she had a "cute little butt." As if that were true praise. If he'd really been paying attention, he might have made a tasteful remark like complimenting her suit or her general appearance, not commenting on the size of her bum.

Irritating man, she thought as she "accidentally" placed her hand on top of the gimmee cap and squashed it flat.

BY THE TIME HANK DROVE into San Antonio, his head was spinning with details of Belegovian history, social protocol, current European nobility and a hundred other subjects he'd never heard of before. Lady Wendy had taken the opportunity to brief him on these subjects so she could start their "hands-on" instruction once they reached the hotel.

Hands-on, he remembered with a chuckle.

"Something you'd like to share, Mr. McCauley?" she asked from her side of the truck.

"Just thinking about all the stuff you have stored."

"Don't you dare say 'in that pretty little head of yours,'" she said in that upper-class British voice of hers that should have left him chilled. Instead, he felt real warm. Getting hotter by the minute.

"Why, I'm shocked that you'd think such a thing!" he said in mock indignation. "You make me sound like some sexist macho pig."

Lady Wendy sniffed and straightened her spine. "I'm surprised you're even familiar with the feminist slur."

"I do get around," he informed her as they slowed for traffic where I-35 branched off. "By the way, which hotel are we goin' to?"

"The Hyatt Regency," she informed him. "I believe it is on what is called the Riverwalk."

"That's right. Best of all, it's just a block from the Alamo."

"Ah, the Texas landmark."

"Darn right! I take it you've never been."

"This is my first trip to Texas," she said in a tone that implied it would also be her last. She just didn't appreciate the state's wide variety of attractions. Hank felt a moral obligation to change her mind.

"Now, all this learnin' and drivin' has tired me out," he informed her as he took I-37 toward downtown San Antonio. "After we get checked in, I'm gonna need a little nap."

"Absolutely not! We have to begin immediately on fitting the wardrobe, learning the speech, mannerisms and posture of Prince Alexi, and heaven knows what else to get you ready for tomorrow!"

"Princess, if I don't get a few hours of shut-eye, I'm not going to do you a bit of good tomorrow or anytime."

"Perhaps you should have thought of that when you stayed up all night, Mr. McCauley."

He narrowed his eyes and gripped the steering wheel tighter, but he doubted Miss High and Mighty noticed his anger. "Well, I wasn't thinkin' about much but saving Sandstorm's life last night, Lady Wendy," he answered with as little sarcasm as possible. Darn woman probably thought he'd been out drinking and chasing women. "Have you ever seen how much misery a horse can be in when they colic? You would have been walkin' her all night and half the morning, too, if it would have saved her."

"Colic? Like with babies?"

"Yeah, except it's more serious with horses. They get down on the ground, first throw their head toward their bellies, then begin to roll 'cause they're in such pain. They can get their guts all twisted and they'll die. It's not a pretty sight, I'll tell you that."

He exited the freeway and pulled the truck to a stop at the light, which gave him a chance to take a nice, long look at his passenger.

"No, I don't imagine it would be," she said with a little shudder. "I take it your horse is better this morning?"

"She's fine. I dosed her until she was all cleaned out, then—"

Lady Wendy held up a hand. "That's enough detail for me, Mr. McCauley."

Hank chuckled, his anger gone as quickly as it began. The light turned green and he turned right. "The hotel's just a few blocks from here. Do you want me to pull into valet parking?"

"No, we've made arrangements for Prince Alexi to enter through the service entrance."

"But I'm not Prince Alexi yet."

"Yes, but you look enough like him that people may recognize you."

"They might also recognize me from my bronc-riding days."

"Really? Are you somewhat of a celebrity, then?"

Hank chuckled again. "Just if you follow rodeo, Princess."

"Please, stop calling me those ridiculous names. As I explained, I'm not royalty."

"Yeah, but you sure are cute when you're riled," he said with a grin.

"I assure you, Mr. McCauley, I've never been called 'cute' in my entire life."

As he stopped at the light to go around the block, he looked again at Wendy. She had a real aristocratic face, kind of narrow with what might be called sharp features. Her biggest assets, in his practiced opinion, were her eyes. He imagined they could get real warm and pretty, with the topaz color and golden highlights. But she didn't use them to flirt. As a matter of fact, she didn't play up any of her features, even that pale, pretty English complexion.

"I think you might be real cute if you'd smile more often."

"I smile."

"Naw, I'm not talkin' about one of those stingy little polite smiles. I'm talkin' about a big old, happy-to-be-alive kind of smile."

He suspected she was blushing, because she looked down at her hands and fiddled with the buttons on her too-heavy suit jacket. "I don't think we should be discussing my smile."

"Why?" He snapped his fingers, getting her attention. "Oh, I get it. You've got that British problem I heard about. I'm sure sorry, Lady Wendy."

"What British problem?" she asked, obviously irritated at his teasing.

"I'm sure sorry I didn't notice it earlier," he whispered, then paused dramatically. "Bad teeth."

He heard her cry of indignation as he pulled to a stop in front of the hotel. "I most assuredly do *not* have bad teeth!"

"Really? Let me see." He leaned toward her.

"Mr. McCauley! Please, I'm not one of your horses!"

"Come on, now, Lady Wendy. Just open up a little and let me see."

"You are incorrigible."

She sounded offended, but he detected a hint of amusement under her starchy facade. "I know I am. It's part of my charm."

She tried harder not to smile.

Hank grinned. "You know you want to show me your pearly whites."

"I'll have you know my mum and dad spent a fair amount on my teeth."

"Yeah? Mine, too. I was always busting out a tooth or chipping one when I got thrown."

"I've never had a chipped tooth."

"Really? They can be pretty sexy."

She sucked in a breath, her topaz eyes suddenly warm. As a matter of fact, the whole inside of the truck seemed to have warmed up considerably. "How?"

He leaned a bit closer. "'Cause you can run your tongue over that little ol' chip."

"Why would that be sexy?" she whispered.

"Maybe I wasn't makin' myself clear. I meant if *you* were kissing *me,* you could run your tongue over that chip. Of course, you'd have to search really long and hard, 'cause it's been fixed for years."

"I see," she said, staring at his mouth.

He couldn't stand it a moment longer. He stretched his arm across the space dividing them, held the back of her head in one hand and kissed her while her lips were parted in surprise. He didn't intend to take advantage of her shock, but her mouth was as sweet as Texas in springtime, and her lips were as soft as bluebonnet petals. His tongue touched hers, then retreated to trace the shape of her teeth—teeth he'd already noted were pearly white and straight as could be. When she moaned, he cupped her cheek with his other hand and deepened the kiss.

Behind them, a car horn honked. Shaking, she pulled away.

"I think you're right," he said, struggling to keep his voice light. "There doesn't seem to be anything at all wrong with your mouth." Or her almost innocent, tentative kiss.

"I'm certainly glad to hear that," she said, her

voice thin and shaky. "Perhaps we should just forget this ever happened, Mr. McCauley."

"I think you should call me Hank," he said as he pulled his hand—and her barrette—away from her hair. He used his fingers to pull the silky length over her shoulders. "There."

"What are you doing?"

"Nobody in his right might would believe that Hank McCauley would check into a hotel with a woman who has her hair all scraped back like yours was. Now you look more...presentable."

"There was nothing wrong with how I looked before!"

"Not for everyday stuff, but checking into a hotel with a man? Naw, you just didn't look right for that."

"Mr. McCauley, we are supposed to be at the service entrance so Prince Alexi can go immediately to his room via the back elevator." Her voice rose and got a little bit higher with each word. She gazed outside, panic setting in at the crowded hotel entrance.

"But I'm Hank McCauley, rodeo star, not Prince Alexi, major pain in the—never mind. Point is, no one's going to believe I'm the prince yet." He put the truck into gear and edged toward valet parking. "Besides, how are we gonna explain my truck around back? Your driver probably has his hands full getting that valet guy settled inside." He pulled out his wallet, spotting a five he could give as a tip. "I'm going to have these nice young men park the dually someplace where I can get to it."

"Are you planning on going somewhere?" she asked, trying to finger-comb her hair.

He reached over and ruffled the glossy reddish-brown strands again. "After that kiss? I don't think so,'' he said, grinning at her flushed, confused expression.

He didn't intend to kiss her again, but she didn't know that. He kind of liked the idea that she was just as out of kilter as he was. He knew he was her means to an end, but that didn't mean everything had to be all serious and secretive. After all, light, fun relationships with women were the only ones he'd allowed himself in six long years.

Lady Wendy didn't need to know that either.

BEFORE GWENDOLYN COULD come up with any more coherent arguments for using the service entrance, Hank McCauley had placed a cowboy hat on his head, jumped down, grinned at the parking attendant and walked around the truck toward her. Good heavens! What was the man thinking? They couldn't just march in the front door and—

"Get your pretty little self on down here, darlin'," he ordered with a smile. As soon as she unfastened the seat belt, he grabbed her around the waist and swung her to the pavement. Before she got her balance, he'd retrieved his carryall and grasped her arm. "I just can't wait to get checked in to our room."

"Really!"

"Yeah, really," he said with a wink, making the two closest luggage handlers grin widely.

"Nice to see you again, Mr. McCauley," one of them called out.

"Good to be here, Ramon."

She looked around, half expecting to see a dozen paparazzi ready to snap their photo. The headlines tomorrow would read "Prince Seduces PR Lady at San Antonio Hotel." King Wilheim would have a coronary. But no one was there except bellhops and other people checking into or out of the hotel. As a matter of fact, no one paid them much attention except the parking attendants.

"They know you at this hotel?" Gwendolyn whispered as they swooshed through the revolving door. "Why didn't you say something?"

"You didn't ask," the irritating man replied.

She wanted to stamp her foot, frown and fume, but they were traveling through a spacious lobby toward the check-in desk. "How am I going to explain your presence here?" she asked, hoping the multitude of large plants and columns hid their arrival from most of the people inside the hotel.

"Just go on and check in. I'm going to make a little detour to the gift shop," he said, nodding toward the glassed-in store just off the lobby. "Come get me when you're finished, darlin'," he said before sauntering off in that rolling gait, his hips and long legs moving easily beneath the worn denim.

"Can I help you?" someone on the other side of the desk asked. Gwendolyn blushed, ashamed she'd been caught staring at that exasperating cowboy's...departure.

"Yes," she said crisply, pushing her hair behind her ears and squaring her shoulders. "I'm Lady Gwendolyn Reed, checking in Prince Alexi's party."

A few minutes later, she found Hank McCauley paying for a large bag of merchandise at the gift shop register. She wondered if he'd charged it to the room or paid cash or used his own personal credit card. Apparently he wasn't as broke as she'd assumed earlier if he could afford to stay at this hotel on a regular basis.

She waited for him beside the door, unwilling to endure more "darlin'" taunts. As if someone would really believe they were a couple!

He gave her a heart-stopping grin. "Ready to go upstairs?"

"Ready to get started with your training?"

He chuckled. "You're tough, you know that?"

"One of us has to be focused on our goal, and since that *is* my job, I'm the one who must insist on staying with our plan." And staying away from any heart-stopping kisses, pats on her "cute little butt," or any further manhandling by this blatantly sexist cowboy.

He was nothing like any Englishman she'd ever known...except in one regard. He obviously thought women should be decorative in and out of the bedroom, and quiet otherwise. His attitude bordered on that of a feudal lord who had his pick of willing wenches. Very soon, Mr. Hank McCauley was going to learn that Lady Gwendolyn Reed was no man's willing wench.

"I still think you haven't thought this through," he said, breaking into her private thoughts. It took her a moment before she realized he meant the substitute prince plan.

"I have very little choice," she said, stopping at the glass-and-brass lift beside an indoor waterway and focusing on her job, not her personal feelings. The water was quite pleasant, but she took little solace in the gurgling sounds. Every minute that passed left her closer to tomorrow's public engagements. She couldn't afford a hint of scandal to reach the ears—or the cameras—of the European paparazzi. Much less reach inside the palace in Belegovia.

Hank McCauley made a halfhearted attempt to hide

a yawn. She supposed he really was tired after staying up all night with the horse. Perhaps she could give him an hour or so for a nap while she arranged her materials. They needed a place setting for a five-course dinner, a sampler of appetizers and a selection of wines. And Milos needed to start measurements in case alterations were necessary to the two suits Hank—as Prince Alexi—would wear tomorrow. Hopefully they wouldn't need to purchase shoes. She doubted San Antonio stores carried the Italian style Alexi preferred.

"If you would like, you may take a nap while I gather what I'll need to continue our training."

The lift doors opened and a family of five exited. She and McCauley entered, only to be followed by an older couple who smiled and nodded. Her substitute prince tipped his hat, just like the hero in a Western movie.

"Whatever works best for you, darlin', he drawled, "but you're always welcome to join me for my nap."

The older couple smiled at the cowboy as if he'd made a profound statement of worldly importance. Gwendolyn closed her eyes and gritted her teeth. Would she ever become accustomed to his outrageous behavior?

Chapter Three

Hank awoke groggy and disoriented, a gentle tapping sound penetrating his foggy brain. He wasn't in his own room back at the ranch, but this big bed was sure comfortable. He stretched, his hands coming in contact with his hat. He'd been wearing it when he'd gone upstairs to the suite. At the Hyatt Regency in San Antonio.

The big suite reserved for Prince Alexi of Belegovia.

The tapping sound stopped. He blinked, focusing on the door. Sure enough, it opened just enough for Lady Wendy to poke her aristocratic nose around the corner. One slim hand held on to the darkly stained wood as if she were dangling for her life.

"Mr. McCauley, are you decent?"

"Darlin', I'm about as decent as I get."

She looked into the room, her eyes reflecting a cautious curiosity. He immediately noticed that she'd pulled her hair back into the severe style she favored.

He couldn't wait to mess it up again.

Whoa! He shouldn't be thinking along those lines. He'd kissed her once, but that needed to be the end of it. Lady Wendy Reed was just a little too sweet, a little too elegant for his white-bread taste. She'd be gone from his life faster than he could say lickety-split.

"I hope you had a pleasant rest, Mr. McCauley, because we need to begin your instruction." He noticed she wasn't looking at him much. He looked down, but sure enough, the buttons on his Levi's were all done up, so that couldn't be it. Either he'd offended her somehow, or she didn't trust herself to watch him. Either way, it didn't bode well for their working relationship.

She sure as hell wasn't calling him "Hank," as he'd asked. She was keeping it real professional with "Mr. McCauley."

He might have overdone the good old boy routine just a bit. Maybe she didn't want to get too familiar with a slightly broken-down bronc rider who had a smart mouth and a low threshold for boredom. With a sigh, he swung his legs over the edge of the bed. "Sure. Let me just splash some water on my face and I'll be right out."

"Very good," she said crisply, pulling the door closed behind her.

She couldn't wait to give him a princely makeover, as if he were inadequate as he was. He didn't like the thought; he didn't appreciate the feeling deep in his gut that to someone like Lady Wendy, he *was* inadequate. If he didn't watch out, he'd work himself into a really lousy mood. That just wouldn't do, since he was in San Antone on someone else's dime. Sure he wanted to learn some fancy manners and figure out what to wear to which event, but he also wanted to have some fun.

Life was too short to spend it all tied up in knots.

He stretched his unreliable back, pleased that his nap hadn't frozen up his often-abused muscles. His old injuries came back to haunt him occasionally, usually at the most inconvenient times. Like when he was trying to impress a woman.

With a big yawn, he made his way into the marble-and-brass bathroom. Time was up; he was about to become Prince Alexi.

SIX HOURS, FIVE COURSES of food, one haircut and manicure, and three alterations of clothing later, Hank was even more tired of this Prince Alexi guy than he'd been this morning. Not only had the prince run off with Kerry Lynn, but he had about the most god-awful boring job in the universe. Smiling, shaking hands, eating, sitting and wearing expensive clothes was about all the prince was good for.

Of course, Hank now understood why Alexi ran off. Only six hours in the prince's shoes—quite literally—and Hank was ready to run screaming from the fancy suite.

"Mr. McCauley, are you listening? The family tree of the royals in Belegovia is very important information."

"I'm sure it is, Lady Wendy, but since I'm going to have laryngitis tomorrow, I can't imagine I'd have to talk to anyone about these relatives of the prince."

"Still, someone may mention one of the dukes or counts, or even their wives. It's important that you are not caught making a mistake regarding your relatives."

"*His* relatives," Hank clarified, scowling at Milos Anatole, who knelt beside him with a mouthful of pins and some chalk. "You know, these pants looked just fine to me."

"Prince Alexi is approximately one half inch taller than you, Mr. McCauley," the uppity, nervous valet announced around the mouthful of pins.

"Yeah, but a half inch? I'm only going to be wearing his things for a few hours."

"It's entirely possible someone could notice that your clothes didn't fit perfectly," Lady Wendy explained.

Hank shook his head. This prince really was a bore. Like the most important thing in the world was whether his pants "broke" at just the proper place above his expensive Italian shoes.

"Who's gonna be lookin' that hard at my pants?" Hank asked, putting both hands on his hips.

Milos frowned up at him. Wendy blinked at him as if he'd said something ridiculous.

"What?"

"Mr. McCauley, the prince is under constant observation by a variety of press. Both legitimate publications and the more irritating paparazzi track his every move. They will be at all the events."

Hank narrowed his eyes. "You never said anything about folks following me around, taking dozens of pictures."

"More like hundreds," Wendy told him in a matter-of-fact voice that for some reason irritated the hell out of him.

Hank squared his shoulders, trying his best to be intimidating. "You owe me."

"You have yet to name your price," she informed him. "Of course, I've already explained that the Belegovian treasury is not an endless well of funds."

"You want me to name my price?"

"Yes, I would appreciate the courtesy. After all, you may decide not to accept a check from the official account. Belegovia is somewhat farther than Oklahoma, as I believe you mentioned—"

"Sarcasm just doesn't suit a sweet lady like you," Hank complained, thoroughly tired of this hotel room and all the facts he'd been forced to memorize. Not to mention a fussy haircut and all those tiny alterations.

"I thought I was being terribly clever."

"Well, you're not," he informed her peevishly. "And as for my fee, I've decided on part of it."

"Part of it? Really, Mr. McCauley, I must insist you decide on a reasonable amount—"

"Tonight. I want to go out with you to the River-walk and have some fun."

She let out a long-suffering sigh. "We are a little busy tonight."

"We're just about finished, that's what we are," he said, his fingers going to the fastening on Prince Alexi's slacks. "We need to get out of here for a few hours. Have a little fun. I'll bet you don't relax enough. A couple of tequila sunrises and a stroll along the river is just what you need."

"I need to succeed in this mission."

"Damn, Lady Wendy, you sound like some secret agent. This isn't life or death, you know. You said we were visiting a children's hospital and a zoo. That means some baby kissin' and smilin' at cuddly little animals."

"No, Mr. McCauley, that is not what this is all about! This is about my career, Prince Alexi's reputation, and quite possibly the future of the monarchy in Belegovia!" Her voice had risen to such a level that

Hank was surprised somebody didn't start pounding on the wall, yelling for them to shut up. Of course, that kind of thing didn't happen in these fancy suites like it did in the cheap motels he'd stayed at while he was on the circuit. Since he'd retired, he'd gotten used to some of the finer things in life, like nice hotels with thick terry cloth towels and twenty-four-hour room service.

"That does it," he announced, batting Milos's hands away from the crease in the slacks. "We're getting out of here."

"Haven't you been listening? We must succeed. You must be accepted as Prince Alexi!"

"I can't do my best work if I'm all stressed out," he said, shaking his head. "You need to get out of those stuffy clothes and into something more comfortable. I've got a hankerin' for a cold beer and some hot salsa."

"Mr. McCauley, we are not going out on the town!"

"Sure we are. It's part of my fee. Look in that bag over there on the couch. I bought you a T-shirt that's just what you need for strollin' along the river on a real pretty night like this."

Lady Wendy ran her hands through her hair, loosening several strands. Hank smiled to himself. She was too easy to rile, too predictable for her own good. All he had to do was push her buttons and she got all huffy. If there was ever a woman who needed to relax and have some fun, she was Lady Wendy.

Besides, no one should visit San Antonio and miss the Riverwalk.

"You'd better run and change," he told her, his hands resting on the waistband of Prince Alexi's slacks. "In about ten seconds I'm gonna be pretty near naked. Now, I don't mind if you don't," he said, easing the zipper lower, "but I figure a lady with your sensibilities wouldn't want to see my beat up ol' body."

"Mr. McCauley, please! We don't have time for fun."

He let pass her unintentional implication that seeing his "beat up old body" would be fun. He walked a fine line—too much teasing and she'd get real mad. "Well, we need to make some, then. I just can't tolerate the thought of you missin' the Riverwalk, much less the Alamo. Why, it's a national shrine!"

"If I promise to come back and visit Texas another time, will you continue working?"

Hank shook his head as he finished unzipping the slacks. "I'd like to believe you, Lady Wendy, but I just can't. I know how busy you career women are. You can't guarantee that you'll make it back to Texas. It's my duty to make sure you see as much of it as possible."

"It's my job to make sure you can pass as Prince Alexi."

"Unless you're ready to compare more than accents and clothes between Prince Alexi and me, you'd better get on out of this room and change into that T-shirt." He lowered the slacks a couple of inches, revealing white briefs.

"Is there no way to talk you out of this insanity?" she asked, blushing a nice pink and staring at the framed artwork over the couch.

"Nope."

She closed her eyes and sighed. Hank hid his smile. He was enjoying this way too much. He couldn't wait to see what Lady Wendy was like after a couple of tequila sunrises and a little two-stepping.

Grabbing the bag containing the pretty Texas T-shirt he'd picked out earlier, she stalked across the room like some British general going to battle. "We'll go to this Riverwalk for one hour," she said, obviously trying to compromise. "I suppose you do deserve a little time off for being such a good sport."

"With an attitude like that, we're bound to have a good time," he said with a chuckle.

GWENDOLYN COULDN'T remember ever being this frustrated and confused. Hank McCauley was the most exasperating, most difficult man she'd had the misfortune to meet. First, he'd insisted on driving his own vehicle—a monstrously large truck, no less. Then he'd driven right up to the front portico of the hotel, despite her instructions to go to the service entrance. He'd kissed her quite deliberately so she'd appear more like one of the women he preferred—except she knew she didn't look a thing like the busty, flirtatious young tarts who flocked to such testosterone-rich cowboys. He'd needed a nap once they were checked in. Now, after only several hours of fittings, a haircut and lessons, he needed a little holiday on this Riverwalk!

"Damn you, Prince Alexi," she muttered under her breath. "I hope you're having a perfectly miserable time, wherever you are."

If he were having a terrible time with his truck-stop waitress, he would end his trip promptly. Everything would return to normal and her job would not be in jeopardy. She would not retreat to England in disgrace to face her overly critical father, who believed she should find a titled, moneyed peer and settle down to a life of charitable works and social engagements, and produce her husband's heir and a spare.

The key word there was *settle*. She had no intention of giving up her career to fit the image of what her stuffy, antiquated father thought was proper for an English lady.

She lifted the soft T-shirt from the bag. A pristine white background held a line of blue flowers—she supposed they were the famed Texas bluebonnets she'd seen on various publications—and a prettily lettered "Texas" in green below. The shirt was certainly a far cry better than some she'd seen—and even imagined Mr. McCauley preferring—which featured ugly animals called armadillos and crude sayings regarding beer, sex and other suggestive activities.

Perhaps Hank McCauley wasn't quite as bad as she'd assumed when she'd first heard the term *retired rodeo cowboy* used to describe him. Or when she'd been told he lived on a ranch outside a small town called Ranger Springs. Or when he'd come to the door dressed only in a pair of nearly indecent jeans.

Heat suffused her cheeks as she remembered how he'd looked when she'd first met him, just out of his shower. Lean and sculpted with impressive muscles and smooth, tanned skin, he could have appeared on an ad for Texas, cowboys or anything else he'd wanted to endorse.

In the suite, he'd made a remark about his "beat-up body," but Gwendolyn hadn't noticed any scars or deformities—at least from the waist up. What was he hiding below the waist of his trousers?

More heat. She had to stop thinking about Hank McCauley's assets. She had to forget the line of white briefs that had appeared when he threatened to lower his slacks.

At least she knew the answer to the question, boxers or briefs?

In her many years of acquaintance with Prince Alexi, she'd never speculated on his underwear. She had no idea what he preferred, nor would he ever show her his preference by lowering his trousers in her presence. He was too much a gentleman.

Her father was a gentleman, and look at what a stuffy bore he was.

Gwendolyn felt like clamping a hand over her mouth for even thinking such a thought. Prince Alexi was not like her father. Hank McCauley was not more exciting than either of the men. He was just… different. More difficult. More…male.

They were going out for one hour, she decided as she unbuttoned her silk blouse. She'd wear the T-shirt to make Hank McCauley happy, she'd even take a sip of one of those tequila sunrises he'd mentioned earlier. But she was absolutely not going dancing.

She sincerely doubted he knew how to waltz or foxtrot—or any of the other ballroom dances she'd learned as the daughter of an earl—and she refused to make a fool of herself attempting one of those fast and complicated western steps she'd seen in movies and on the telly. No matter what he said or how persuasive he was, she would *not* be humiliated on the dance floor.

"HANG ON, LADY WENDY. It's time to twirl again."

"No more twirling!" she managed to gasp as her arms circled his neck. "I believe I'm quite dizzy."

"But you're doin' such a good job of polishing my belt buckle."

"What?"

"Dancin' real close, darlin'," he replied, his breath a whisper against her ear. The sensation made her even more dizzy and she sagged in his arms.

"You should have told me you couldn't handle your liquor," Hank said.

Somewhere between a deliciously decadent appetizer called nachos supreme and a wonderfully tasty drink called a tequila sunrise, her pretend prince had become Hank rather than Mr. McCauley. She heard the humor in his voice but couldn't muster the outrage she should be feeling. He'd been teasing her unmercifully for the past half hour, but instead of becoming angry, she was beginning to find his remarks witty.

She'd definitely had too many sips of the sweet yet tangy drink. Hank McCauley was bossy, opinionated and manipulative. He was also the sexiest man she'd ever met…and he made her feel like dancing.

She tried to unwind her arm so she could see her wristwatch, but Hank simply pulled her tighter. She gave up with a sigh, knowing she wasn't going to win this battle any more than she'd won the rest of their skirmishes.

As soon as she'd dressed in the T-shirt and a casual skirt, Hank had knocked on her door. He'd grinned his approval, grabbed her hand and guided her to the elevator. He'd given her a history lesson of the Riverwalk. She'd learned how San Antonio had taken a run-down, foul-smelling river and turned it into one of the best-known attractions in Texas. When they'd walked out of the Hyatt Regency, they'd entered another world. The humidity of the river provided a perfect backdrop to the tropical foliage and abundant flowers. Fun-loving tourists crowded the sidewalk. To Gwendolyn's surprise, there was no fence or railing. The concrete merely stopped at the water, which was really a dredged-out canal.

No telling how many people had sipped too many alcoholic drinks and fallen into the river! Hank had merely grinned and told her it was only three or four feet deep, so she didn't need to worry.

The idea of *not* worrying about tumbling into the murky river was as foreign to her as thinking of Hank McCauley as Prince Alexi.

"We should be going back to the hotel," she said. She wasn't sure when exactly she'd lost control—whether it was when she'd first knocked on his screen door or when she'd decided to accompany him to the Riverwalk—but she was certain he was now making decisions for them both. While that realization should have caused panic, at the moment she only felt an increasing interest in what he would insist upon next.

"With any other woman, I'd take that as an invitation. But I kind of doubt you were asking me up to your room, were you?"

"Of course not!" she managed to squeal as he steered them across the floor between some very young dancers and a middle-aged pair. How he avoided the other couples was a complete mystery. "We barely know each other."

"How much more do you need to know?"

"Well, I… That's not what I meant."

"You sure are cute when you're flustered, Lady Wendy."

Instead of feeling outraged, she had the insane urge to giggle. British peers did not giggle. She could almost hear her father's censure, all the way across the "pond."

"Oh, pooh," she whispered as they neared the table where more drinks awaited.

"What's wrong?"

"Nothing. I was just thinking about my father."

"It's not good to tell a guy that he reminds you of your father."

"Oh, you don't! Believe me, two men could not be more different than you and the Earl of Epswich." She desperately needed to change the subject before Hank started asking her more personal questions that she had no intention of answering—yet might find herself responding to, anyway.

"That chap over there is how I imagined most Texans," Gwendolyn remarked, nodding toward a couple in fancy Western attire gliding across the dance floor. "He's big and brash and bold. His hat alone is as large as a brolly. Do you think he drinks as much beer as his physique indicates?" The middle-aged man sported an enormous beer belly that didn't keep him from holding his partner, a rather petite woman near his own age, close against his torso. She wore a full denim skirt, a Western shirt and boots that matched his outfit perfectly.

"If you're asking me about the size of his beer belly, I'd have to say no. It takes more than beer to grow one that large. I'd say he had some help from chicken-fried steak and homemade pie à la mode."

Gwendolyn couldn't help herself. A great gasp of laughter gurgled up from inside her, erupting in a completely unladylike display of mirth. She tried to control herself—her mouth was too wide for grinning, her cheeks too dimpled—but the effort left her with watering eyes and a sore jaw.

"So you can smile," Hank remarked, leaning close across the small table. His finger touched the corner of her mouth, making her breath catch and her grin fade. "I was wonderin'. And I can see now that there's nothin' wrong with your teeth. I guess I made a big mistake thinkin' you were tryin' to hide ugly yellow chompers."

"Chompers?" She couldn't control another giggle. "Really, you are too absurd. Wherever do you get these ideas, not to mention these sayings?"

"Comes with the territory, darlin'," he said with a grin. "Kind of like Resistol hats and beer bellies."

She got the laughter under control. "I thought cowboys wore Stetsons."

"Not really, at least not for everyday. That just sounds good. We also don't wear ten-gallon hats, tuck our jeans into our boots or ride horses down main streets."

"And you certainly don't have a beer belly." The words burst forth before she could control her errant mouth. What was it about this man that caused her good sense to flee like tender petals in a March wind?

"Nope," he said, running his hand over his flat stomach as he grinned in a way that made her want to smile. "Don't plan on getting one, either."

"I'm certainly glad to hear that," she whispered, leaning toward him with an increasing lack of restraint. "I'd hate to have to compare yours to that chap's over there." She pulled back, startled at the way her mouth was running ahead of her brain. "Not that I would…or is that something men do? Compare the size of their—"

"Lady Wendy! I'm shocked you'd think such a thing. We use the same standard as the rest of the U.S. of A. to judge manliness." He paused, grinning slowly, making her heart race in anticipation of the next outrageous remark he was about to make. The next remark she'd prompted him to make.

Ridiculous. She'd never encouraged such behavior before.

"No," he continued, "here in Texas we don't flaunt the size of our beer bellies. We use something far more personal."

She felt like crawling beneath the tiny table. "Why don't we forget I brought up this subject?"

"And miss letting you in on some cultural learning? No, you have to know that we judge a man by the size of his—"

"Mr. McCauley!"

"—truck."

She leaned back in her chair, her eyes blinking in disbelief, before the laughter bubbled forth once more to overwhelm her senses.

HANK FELT THE EVENING had been an unqualified success. He'd had a rip-roaring good time showing Lady Wendy the Riverwalk and one of his favorite honky-tonks. She'd enjoyed her first tequila sunrise, her first taste of nachos and her first Texas two-step. Although she'd insisted they could only afford one hour away from his princely training, he'd managed to turn one hour into nearly three. At midnight he'd told her good-night at her door, holding her hands and telling her this lapse in her precious timetable wasn't her fault. He'd told her that he would have taken her to the

Alamo if he hadn't been so intimidated by her need for "shedyules."

Lord knows, she couldn't be blamed for his faults. He was a bounder, as his dearly departed grandma used to say. He loved to tease and party and dance. He loved to make women smile as much as he loved to hold them in his arms. Lady Wendy was a particular challenge due to her strict British upbringing and inflated sense of duty, but when she did unwind...shoot, boy, howdy!

Hank pulled off his boots and stretched out on the bed. He stuffed a few pillows behind him before reaching for the notes Lady Wendy and Milos Anatole had given him earlier in the evening. Forms of address, proper etiquette, drafts of speeches and a schedule of events had been stressed for several hours while Milos had cut his hair "to a civilized length," smeared some sweet-smelling lotion on his face "to eliminate ruddiness," and fitted him with "a proper wardrobe." Hank supposed Wendy thought he hadn't been paying close attention to all her instructions, but he had.

Studying an hour or so more wouldn't hurt. He had no intention of embarrassing her or jeopardizing the monarchy of Belegovia—whatever that meant.

Even more now than when she'd shown up on his porch, he wanted to help her succeed. For reasons he couldn't comprehend, saving Prince Alexi's sorry butt was important to her. She'd said there was nothing going on between her and the royal bore, but Hank wasn't convinced. Maybe when she looked at him or danced with him, she imagined she was with the prince. Maybe she'd had a royal crush for years.

How in the hell, Hank wondered, could he be jealous of a man he didn't know? Prince Alexi had rubbed him the wrong way from the moment Wendy had told him about the prince running off with Kerry Lynn. Not that he was jealous because of Kerry Lynn. No, as much as he hated to admit it, Hank knew he was jealous because Wendy had spent so much of her time with the prince. A man who apparently had everything but common sense...and maybe common decency. Why in the world would he leave Lady Wendy—a long-time friend and employee—in the lurch to pursue a selfish desire for a little fun? How could he do that to a fine woman like her?

Hank knew he shouldn't be thinking about Wendy's personal situation, but there was just something about her that brought out his protective instincts. She was a foreigner in this land, far away from home and charged with a huge responsibility. She had a lot of guts, which he admired in anyone, but more than that, she was as sexy as hell for a prim-and-proper English lady.

For one thing, she had a beautiful mouth, wide and as inviting as all get out. Her teeth were straight and white, and when he'd kissed her, she'd tasted like heaven on earth. When she grinned really big, like when he'd teased her after their last dance, he'd discovered two dimples that made him want to keep her smiling for a long time. Which wasn't going to happen. She was here in the U.S. temporarily; he didn't plan to leave Texas unless he had to on business.

"Doesn't matter," Hank muttered to himself. Wendy was fun to tease, exciting in an innocent manner and admirable in her dedication to her job, but she was really just another woman who was using him to get what she wanted.

Hell, he didn't hold that against her. He'd agreed to

the job for his own reasons. He was learning some manners, getting some exposure to fine clothes and shoes, so he couldn't complain. His ranch was in good hands for a few days and he was having fun.

He reached for the sheaf of papers, shaking off his morose thoughts for more practical matters. Tomorrow he wouldn't be meeting any dukes, earls or barons, but he still had to look the role of a prince.

"Piece of cake," he murmured. After all, he'd been playing the role of a devil-may-care rodeo champion for most of his adult life.

Chapter Four

"You look like you just swallowed a bad oyster," Hank whispered as they walked through the brass-and-glass doors of the hotel for the first of two events on the "prince's" agenda that day.

Wendy swallowed the imaginary lump, using every ounce of willpower to keep walking toward the Land Rover. She now knew what the condemned must feel like, going bravely toward their fate when their insides had turned to mush and their legs quivered like jelly.

"If I'm a bit nervous, I'm sure you can understand why."

"Too much partyin' last night, Lady Wendy?" he whispered so only she could hear as they passed several attentive bellhops.

"Not enough practicing, Mr.—Your Highness," she replied, smiling at the beaming bell captain who had opened the door of the vehicle. To the left, a few paparazzi snapped some photos, but no one seemed too concerned about the prince's first appearance in San Antonio this morning.

At least they weren't suspicious *yet*.

She nodded toward Hank McCauley, since as the prince he was expected to enter the Land Rover first.

He frowned a bit—no doubt that strange Texas chivalry he practiced—because he believed in "ladies first." Well, he would just have to become accustomed to acting as royalty. She wasn't about to cater to his whims when she couldn't understand more than a pinch of his customs, phrases or humor.

But he certainly looked the part of the prince this morning, from his neatly styled hair to the designer suit. No royal had ever looked more appealing than this Texas cowboy. Gwendolyn suddenly realized that she could just as easily envision him in Prince Alexi's suit as in Hank's own black Stetson. Or whatever brand of hat he'd mentioned last evening. Some of the details were a tiny bit fuzzy—or perhaps she'd subconsciously tried to forget how they'd laughed and danced far too late into the night.

"Let's be off, Mr. Boedecker," she ordered once they were settled inside the vehicle. At least the darkly tinted windows kept the inquisitive away so they could have a much-needed *professional* conversation on the way to the zoo.

"You must remember—" she started to say.

"That suit sure looks pretty on you, Lady Wendy," Hank interrupted.

Gwendolyn snapped her mouth closed when she realized she must resemble a dead fish. She smoothed the skirt of her light-weight teal-green suit. "Thank you, but, Mr. McCauley, we have little time. Let's get down to business."

"You're the boss," he replied with a heart-stopping grin.

"For one thing, don't smile in such an exuberant manner. Prince Alexi has much more…controlled expressions."

Hank shook his head and frowned. "This guy just keeps getting better and better."

Gwendolyn ignored his sarcasm. "You remember the words we practiced this morning?"

"How could I forget? I had 'splendid' coffee, 'magnificent' eggs and 'outstanding' toast."

Gwendolyn frowned. "Those are exactly the types of comments Prince Alexi will make regarding the various wildlife he will encounter at the zoo."

Hank leaned closer and murmured, "My idea of wildlife is a little different. Dancing the two-step with a pretty lady, for example."

A discreet chuckle from the driver's seat caused heat to flare in Gwendolyn's cheeks. "Would you please stop making such comments? We will be at the zoo in minutes. This first event is extremely important."

"Lady Wendy, you worry too much. I'm going to have laryngitis and I'll barely be able to praise all those wild animals we're about to visit."

"Yes, but make the curators understand how pleased you are to be there. And remember to smile and wave at the crowd in the manner we practiced."

"I know," he sighed. "I swear, I waved and smiled myself to sleep last night."

Another chuckle, this time louder, came from the driver.

"Mr. Boedecker, are we nearing our destination?" Gwendolyn asked in a tone she hoped conveyed her disapproval of his eavesdropping.

"Yes, ma'am," he replied. "I think we're on the right course."

This time Hank chuckled. Gwendolyn shook her head. Men. No, *Texans*. She'd never understand them.

HANK THOUGHT HE'D DONE a pretty good job at the zoo. Lots of smiling, nodding and walking around looking pretty darn official in that nice suit belonging to Prince Alexi. Of course, it was way too hot for Texas in May, but Hank had tried his best to keep cool. Think cool thoughts. Definitely not think about Lady Wendy.

Oh, she looked as cool as a shady lake on a summer evening, all dressed in green with her ivory skin and reddish brown hair. And she tried her best to maintain that crisp English look with the occasional slightly raised eyebrow and tight little smiles. But he knew she could be clever, funny and sexy—maybe more than she realized herself. He was a bit surprised how much he wanted to see more of that side of her.

"This appearance will be a bit harder," she said, breaking into his thoughts. He sure wished she'd watch her choice of words. *Hard* described him far too often in the last twenty-four hours.

"What's different about it? Other than the critters will have two legs instead of four?"

He could tell Wendy was hiding a smile. "For one thing, we'll be surrounded by more people on a much closer basis. You'll be expected to make impromptu comments about more than the magnificence of a particular species." She paused, sitting up straighter on her side of the Land Rover. "I believe I've come up with a solution."

"No more laryngitis? I'm not quite ready to try out my English accent yet."

"Of course not. What I had in mind was for you to pretend to whisper your comments to me, and I would convey the appropriate response to the audience."

"So basically, you want me to whisper sweet nothings into your ear."

"No! I mean, you only need to pretend to whisper the comments I'll be making. No one will need to overhear us."

"Oh, this just keeps getting better," he said, leaning closer. "I can whisper whatever I want...or nothing at all?"

Lady Wendy sucked in a breath, tensing up so much he thought she might turn blue. "I would certainly appreciate it if you'd keep your remarks civil and professional. Prince Alexi's public image, and indeed, the future of Belegovia, depends on how effective these personal appearances are."

"Well, I sure wouldn't want to hurt the prince's public image, especially when he's off gallivanting across our fair state with Kerry Lynn." He frowned, remembering the possessive way he felt about the Ranger Springs native who waited tables out on I-35 to help support her family. Kind of like an older brother, which Kerry Lynn didn't have to defend her. "Did I mention that I'm going to have a serious talk with this prince when he shows up? If he's hurt Kerry, he's gonna learn a bit about frontier justice."

"Mr. McCauley, certainly you're not threatening Prince Alexi!"

"I sure as hell am. He can't fly in here with that jet you said he has and fancy wardrobe and take advantage of our women."

"I thought Ms. Jacks was no longer your girlfriend."

"I'm not talkin' about that. Texas men defend all the women of our state, not just those we might be related to or involved with."

"I certainly can't believe that Prince Alexi would do anything to harm Ms. Jacks."

"I'm just tellin' you that he'd better not be messin' with her feelings."

"Prince Alexi is always honest and straightforward in his relationships."

Hank narrowed his eyes and glared at Wendy. "I thought you said there's nothing goin' on between the two of you."

"There's not! We've been friends for years, before his father resumed the throne of Belegovia. We attended school together in England from our early years."

Hank studied her. She seemed to be telling the truth. That didn't mean she didn't want to have more than a friendly relationship with the prince. What little girl didn't dream of becoming a princess when she grew up? But he had to take Lady Wendy at her word…at least for now.

But if that prince had messed with Kerry Lynn… Hank knew he couldn't think about that right now without getting madder than a hornet.

Pete Boedecker drove under the portico of the hospital, effectively cutting off all conversation about the prince and thoughts of him taking advantage of relative innocents.

"Remember," Lady Wendy ordered in that aristocratic voice of hers, "when you are asked a question, simply lean toward me and pretend to whisper your response into my ear. I'll take care of everything else."

"Sure thing, Lady Wendy. I aim to please."

"His Highness, Prince Alexi, regrets that he will be unable to answer your questions directly, as he has been advised not to use his voice until he is feeling...more like himself again.''

Gwendolyn thought she felt a shudder—rather like someone suppressing a chuckle—from Hank McCauley, but when she looked at him, he maintained a carefully blank, if cordial, expression.

In the audience, a half-dozen local reporters and several paparazzi she recognized from other events occupied the first row of the seats, while hospital personnel filled the remaining chairs. Two video cameras were operated near the wall, while several photographers crouched on the floor near the journalists. All in all, this was a good turnout for a local event. Given the real prince's absence, perhaps no reporters would have been better, but Hank was performing with aplomb so far.

''What's the most interesting thing the prince has seen on his trip?'' one of the reporters asked.

Hank leaned close and whispered, ''That would be Lady Wendy hauling her cute little butt up into my pickup truck.''

Gwendolyn, by force of will, kept her eyes from popping open or choking on her outrage. She swallowed, then smiled for the audience. ''The prince says that he has enjoyed meeting the wonderful variety of people in Texas, both in big cities and small towns.''

''How does Texas compare to Belegovia?''

''I'm not real sure, since I've never been there,'' Hank whispered, his breath sending shivers down her neck, ''but I think it's a lot hotter here. Don't you think so, Lady Wendy?''

Gwendolyn coughed discreetly and answered,

"Prince Alexi says the weather is quite a bit warmer here."

A few members of the press and the hospital officials chuckled. Another person asked, "What other plans does the prince have for his visit?"

Hank leaned even closer and whispered, "I'd like to take you dancing again in the moonlight. I'd like to hear you laugh again. I'd like to kiss your—"

Gwendolyn bolted upright in her chair, knowing she looked foolish but unable to stop herself. "Prince Alexi will be returning to Belegovia this weekend, after a brief visit to Austin for dinner with the governor and perhaps to Crawford."

"Then he's going to meet with the president on his ranch?"

Gwendolyn didn't wait for Hank to whisper anything this time. "Those plans have not been finalized, and of course are dependent on the president's schedule. Now, if you will excuse us, Prince Alexi needs to rest his voice. The doctor has prescribed some particularly vile medicine to cure his problem," she added with a saccharine smile for him.

"Touché," Hank whispered in her ear. "Are we going to play doctor when we get back to the hotel?"

Gwendolyn burst from her seat. "Thank you for coming today." When Hank stood beside her and leaned forward, she knew she wasn't going to appreciate his remark. His childishly—no, scratch that—his immature sexual innuendo. She moved out of range, sweeping her hand forward in an effort to show him he was to proceed her out of the seating area.

They made their way out of the small conference room after posing for a few more photos. Earlier, hospital officials had discussed their ongoing programs in the treatment of childhood disease, announcing a grant by Prince Alexi for a new, state-of-the-art diagnostic machine. No one realized that he'd donated the funds from his personal account, not from the royal treasury. Although his impromptu trip with the truck-stop waitress had shown his impulsive side, he was also, in Gwendolyn's opinion, a very generous and thoughtful man.

He certainly didn't make inappropriate sexual remarks in public settings. Or anywhere, to Gwendolyn's knowledge. Not that she was privy to his personal liaisons.

Within minutes they were whisked through the quiet, sterile corridors of the hospital toward the portico where the Land Rover awaited. Hank had relaxed into his role, shaking the hand of the hospital administrator before exiting the building, rasping out yet another ''splendid'' in the British accent they'd perfected just that morning.

''Back to the hotel, Mr. Boedecker.''

They settled into the seats, both breathing a sigh of relief. Or at least Gwendolyn assumed that was Hank's response until he turned to her with an unholy gleam in his eyes.

''Damn, Lady Wendy, you got me all hot and bothered at that press conference. I had no idea you cool Brits could heat up the room so fast.''

''What—what in the world are you talking about?''

''All that prim-and-proper behavior. All those clever answers. I found that downright sexy.''

The Land Rover turned left, throwing Gwendolyn off balance—just like Hank's remarks. She braced her hand on the seat and faced him. ''Sexy! Do you have any idea how I had to control myself to keep from…from striking you? And I am not a violent person!''

Hank leaned closer and grinned. ''Got you all hot and bothered, too, didn't I?''

''Most certainly not!''

''Liar, liar, pants on fire.''

''Oh, you—'' She gripped the seat as they entered the fast-moving motorway. Now he was making comments about her undergarments.

''Now, don't get all prissy on me again. I'm just tryin' to get a few things straight between us.''

''You are trying to irritate me! You are trying to make me lose my composure in a public setting, but you're not going to be successful. No matter what you do, I will not become a victim of your immature pranks.''

''Oh, really,'' he said, and she immediately realized she'd waved a red flag in front of a dangerous bull. A paw-the-earth, fire-breathing beast. *Bullheaded* was more like it, but she didn't know how to take back her words without apologizing, which she wasn't about to do since she was right.

Before she could pull her composure about her like a shield, his hand came up and cradled her jaw. She could only gape as his lips descended. She could only hold her breath as his mouth settled on hers, lightly, more gently than she would have expected.

As if she could ever have expected *this*.

She closed her eyes as he coaxed a response she didn't believe she was giving. As he cupped the back of her skull and tilted her head to the side. As her lips parted ever so slightly.

The Land Rover jerked to a near-stop, throwing

Gwendolyn forward. Hank immediately grabbed her arms, steadying her on the seat.

Oh, if only she felt steady.

She drew in a shaky breath. "Thank you, but I must ask that you unhand me."

A smile curved his sensual lips. "Unhand you? I'll bet no one has said that since some damsel in distress in a 1940s movie."

Gwendolyn settled back on her side of the seat. Way back. Near the door. "I don't know why you…did that, but I must insist you not repeat your behavior. We will be working together quite closely for the next few days in purely a professional situation."

Hank leaned closer, his expression not quite pleasant and more than a little tense. "I wasn't the only one doin' the kissin'."

"Have you ever noticed your accent becomes more pronounced when you're trying to convince someone you're right?"

"Nope. And don't avoid the issue. You kissed me back and you know it."

"You took me by surprise," Gwendolyn claimed, looking away from his beautiful mouth to the traffic ahead of them. Did Prince Alexi have such sculpted, sensitive lips?

"Darlin', I'll take you any way I can get you."

His outrageous comment made her see red. She turned toward him, sure that he'd be grinning like the fool he was. But he wasn't smiling. He looked serious—far too serious for her peace of mind.

"Mr. McCauley, I must ask you stop making these remarks."

"You can ask all you want, darlin', but some things are just in my nature."

"Yes, I agree you're a natural flirt, Mr. McCauley, but—"

"That's not what I'm talkin' about. I mean it's natural for me to be attracted to a beautiful woman."

"There is no need for flattery, Mr. McCauley. I'm aware I have few of the attributes most men find so attractive."

"Now, that's a bunch of bull, Lady Wendy."

"I don't believe so."

His eyes narrowed in a gesture she now identified as a prelude to dangerous behavior. "As much as you'd like to believe you know just about everything, you're not an expert on that subject."

"I have had other relationships, Mr. McCauley," she informed him, giving him a casual shake of her head as if his oddly endearing flattery didn't affect her at all.

"Yeah? Want to compare notes?"

"Certainly not!" She barely kept the smile off her face at yet another outrageous remark.

"Say, I'm about to starve to death. Why don't we stop and get a bite to eat?"

"We can hardly be seen in a public restaurant as Prince Alexi and Lady Gwendolyn Reed. Lunch is not on our agenda. I planned to order lunch from room service when we return to the hotel."

"Now, I like that hotel just fine, but hotel food is a little like airline food—it's just not the same as goin' out on your own for ribs, barbecue or chicken-fried steak."

"Prince Alexi doesn't eat that type of food."

Hank McCauley leaned closer, a wicked grin on his face. "Yeah, but I do. And I'm just dyin' to see you dig into some of the best ribs in the state of Texas."

"I don't believe I'd like ribs."

"Oh, darlin', I know you will. We just need to get you out of those prissy clothes and into something more comfortable. We'll take the dually and just be Hank McCauley and a lady friend."

"We need to drive to Austin for the next event—a very formal affair tonight."

"I'll be ready for whatever kind of affair you want to have, but you just can't leave the San Antone area without trying the ribs in Boerne."

"Where in the world is Burney?"

"Not far at all. I'll show you on the map. It's a German town spelled b-o-e-r-n-e. Maybe twenty miles or so. Believe me, the food is worth the drive."

"Really," she protested weakly, wishing she could share lunch or dinner with this Texas cowboy at some small town. "I'm sorry, but we need to go over my notes, the social protocol and the people you'll be expected to greet at the event in Austin. There simply isn't time for a side trip to Boerne for ribs."

"I'm real sorry to hear that. Lunch would have been my treat."

She wasn't sure what he meant by that remark, so she let it pass. Asking Hank McCauley to explain his remarks led to some very long and frustrating conversations that occasionally evolved into...inappropriate behavior.

They entered the lobby of the Hyatt with polite nods and a few curious glances. Hank carried off the persona of a prince with admirable grace. Before long they were inside the prince's suite. A blinking red light on the phone flashed like an alarm to Wendy. Who knew to call them here? But then she remembered that Prince Alexi really was out there somewhere; perhaps he'd had a change of heart and was ready to return to his duties.

The thought that she would no longer need Hank McCauley caused a little flutter in her stomach, but she didn't have time to explore the reaction.

She pressed the message button and immediately knew this was not a social call from the prince. After the first few words, she hit the speakerphone button.

"Alexi, this is your father. I have been unable to reach you on your mobile phone. You need to have it repaired immediately." A slight pause made Gwendolyn lean closer. "I have arranged for Contessa Fabiana Luisa di Giovanni to attend the reception in Austin. Since you have been unable to select a bride, I have taken the task upon myself. She is a lovely young lady without any scandal in her past. She would make a suitable princess for Belegovia. You *will* be accommodating to her."

"Damn," Hank muttered behind her.

"I will expect a call later, along with a report on your public appearances today. Goodbye, Alexi."

"I don't suppose there's any doubt who was ordering ol' Alexi around like a naughty schoolboy."

"King Wilheim is rather insistent that Alexi marry soon."

"Poor guy. I sure as heck wouldn't want my daddy to pick out my bride."

"Prince Alexi's sentiments exactly." Gwendolyn turned to face Hank, folding her arms across her chest. "And you are about to have the honor of beginning his courtship of the lovely contessa."

Chapter Five

Hank had never seen so many glasses, forks, spoons and other gadgets that he had no idea what to do with. Well, this is what he'd wanted, wasn't it? To learn how to mix and mingle with wealthy owners, eat at five-star restaurants or attend fancy dinner parties, and generally keep from making a fool of himself in front of the rich and famous.

He'd kind of forgotten why he was pretending to be Prince Alexi last night and during the day today. He'd never admit it to Lady Wendy, but he was enjoying the role of the temporarily semimute prince. Or he had been enjoying it until he'd seen this table setting.

Prince Alexi's valet walked around a serving cart where a variety of covered dishes produced some pretty darn delicious aromas. He stopped at Hank's left and gestured to the array of stemmed glasses hovering around the china plate like attentive soldiers. Beneath the place setting, a snowy white tablecloth that was probably linen had been starched and pressed.

"There will be a different wineglass for each vintage served with a course," Milos Anatole instructed, "plus a goblet for water."

"No iced tea or long necks, hmm?" Hank muttered.

Milos ignored him. "All forks will be used from the outside to inside, in order of the courses, to the left of the plate, with the exception of the dessert flatware, which may be located on top of the place setting. Your butter knife, of course, will be placed horizontally on top of the side plate for rolls."

"Of course."

"Always break your roll into smaller pieces and butter them individually. Never take a bite out of the entire roll."

"Never."

"The finger bowl," Milos said, pointing to the little glass dish that looked like it could hold a child's portion of soup, "may have a curl of lemon or rose petals, but it is used to refresh the fingers between courses."

"I'll try not to get confused and drink it."

Milos rolled his eyes in exasperation, then continued. "It is well known that Prince Alexi prefers the 'Sydney Opera House' folded napkin. After the table is seated, remove the napkin and gently unfold it if there is not an attendant to do so for you."

"Are you saying that people stand around just to unfold my napkin for me? They'd better not try to smooth it over my lap."

What kind of useless guy was this prince? And who could possible know—or care—which type of folded napkin the prince preferred? Hell, Hank always considered it a plus when he had paper napkins at the house instead of using a roll of paper towels.

"That is not their only function, of course. They will also refresh condiments and remove soiled dishes between courses."

"Just so they don't wipe my damned chin between bites."

Milos turned up his pointed nose. "I certainly hope that won't be necessary. Try to remember that the honor of Belegovia and the Ladislas family is at stake."

Hank narrowed his eyes and started to say something sarcastic, but decided against it. After all, it wasn't this little guy's fault that royalty was pretty near useless. "Okay, what's next?"

"If you'll be seated, I'll begin serving."

With a sigh, Hank settled into the fancy chair facing the overwhelming place setting of china, crystal and sterling. He had a feeling he was going to get his not-so-royal knuckles slapped more than once this afternoon.

"Let's begin with caviar and toast."

Hank tried to control his joy as he looked down at the jellied fish eggs. His lip only curled slightly in distaste as he replied, "If you insist."

"YOUR MAJESTY, I'M SORRY that the prince is unable to talk on the phone. He is suffering from a very hoarse voice and has been advised not to speak for a few days."

"What has caused this problem? He was fine when he left Belegovia."

"I'm sure it is nothing too serious. Everything should be back to normal within a few days," she said, crossing her fingers and sending a silent prayer skyward. *Please, let the real prince return soon. I hate lying to everyone.*

"If you would like for me to convey your wishes to the prince, I will do my best to see that everything is taken care of. He was quite excited when we received your message regarding the contessa."

"Excited! I'll remind you that you are speaking to the king, who is also a father. My son is about as excited to marry as the most jaded playboy in Europe. If it were up to him, he would pick a bride when he is on his deathbed, Lord grant that will be many, many years from now."

Gwendolyn understood what King Wilheim meant. Alexi had never been interested in marrying—not when he was a young public school student, an active and popular collegiate, or when he'd gone to the States to attend Harvard for his advanced degree. Even when his father regained the throne and Alexi knew he would be crown prince, he didn't want to think about marrying to continue the royal line. If he were anyone else, people would remark that he simply wasn't the marrying kind.

The rules of others didn't apply to a prince, though, and sooner or later Alexi had to make a choice. Gwendolyn just wondered if the king was going to have to orchestrate the courtship and plan the wedding, or if Alexi would take part at last. She had the sudden image of Alexi running away from the church as his Italian bride waited at the altar.

"Yes, Your Majesty, I see your point. However, the prince is practically a different person now. I'm sure he will enjoy meeting the contessa in Austin tonight."

"I certainly hope you are right. I rely upon you, Lady Gwendolyn, to temper his stubborn behavior. As always, you are a steadying influence on my son, and for that, I am grateful."

She wanted to crawl beneath the desk and hide her head. King Wilheim trusted her to do her job, which was to represent the royal family to the world and promote the interests of Belegovia. On her first trip to the States with Prince Alexi, she'd failed miserably, losing the prince and substituting Hank McCauley, who, quite frankly, was unprepared for attending a dinner at the governor's mansion.

"Thank you, Your Majesty. I will try to be worthy of your kind words."

"I know you will. My son may be somewhat negligent in his duties to the throne, but you are always trustworthy. Good day, Lady Gwendolyn."

She replaced the handset as the line went dead. Oh, heavens. What had she gotten into? What if the king discovered her deception? He would be so disappointed… Her career would be over, since who else would hire the public relations coordinator who lost a prince?

She'd return to England a failure and would be forced to endure the "I told you so" looks of her father and brother. They'd never believed she was capable of succeeding in her chosen career. They'd wanted her to find a husband from the peerage and settle into a moldy mansion somewhere outside London to raise a generation of new peers who could look down their aristocratic noses on the lower orders. The exact kind of people who now supported her family by paying admission to Epswich Manor, their ancestral home. Her father would never admit it, but the country house of the earls of Epswich was now little more than a bed-and-breakfast inn.

"Takin' a little break?" Hank's mellow, deep voice startled her so much she nearly fell out of the desk chair. "Whoa, there," he said, suddenly beside her, his large hands gripping her shoulders. His touch felt so good, so solid, when her world seemed to be spinning out of control. But she couldn't depend on Hank to give a false illusion of safety when he was a part of the deception she was perpetrating.

"Thank you," she said breathlessly as she stepped back. She straightened her suit jacket, which she'd never removed from the events this morning, and smoothed her hair. "I wasn't expecting you so soon."

"I told ol' Milos that if I had to look at another course or taste any more of that rich, fancy food I was going to hurl onto his clean white tablecloth."

Gwendolyn clapped a hand over her mouth to keep from laughing out loud. What Hank said shouldn't have been funny, but he was simply so amusing. His clever comments, unique word choices and Texas accent made her chuckle, even at inappropriate remarks. "I see."

"Did you know that you're supposed to pick up asparagus with your *fingers?* Or that you can eat caviar out of these little pots with tiny spoons?"

Gwendolyn smiled at his outraged expression. "Yes, I believe I had heard that."

"I sure as heck hope we're not served asparagus at the fancy dinner tomorrow night, because my mother would rap my knuckles if I pick up veggies with my fingers."

"I'm sure many people prefer to eat asparagus with a knife and fork."

"Darn right!" he answered indignantly, pacing across the room. He nodded toward the phone. "Did you call the king?"

"Yes, I did."

"And he bought our story about the prince having a sore throat?"

"Yes." The knowledge that Hank had used the word *our* warmed her heart. She was sure that he'd considered this plan completely daft and entirely her responsibility at first. Did she dare hope that he'd become so involved in the subterfuge that he now considered them partners until the real prince surfaced?

"I'm afraid I had to promise the king that you—acting as the prince, of course—would be cordial and welcoming to Contessa di Giovanni."

"As long as I don't have to go beyond kissing her fingers or smiling real politely. I'm willing to start ol' Alexi's courtship, but darned if I'm gettin' personal with a strange foreign woman."

Again, Gwendolyn hid her smile. "So, you don't like foreign women."

Hank narrowed his eyes. "This is a trick question, isn't it?"

"Not really," she replied, walking across the room to the small refrigerator in an armoire. "I simply wondered what your main objection was to the contessa."

"I'm not objectin' to her, just warning you that my 'services' don't extend to the bedroom."

Gwendolyn grabbed a bottle of water with a death grip. "The thought never crossed my mind! I assure you, that will not be an issue. The prince and the contessa have yet to meet."

"I've heard some of you European aristocrats are pretty wild. I didn't want to give you the wrong idea."

"Mr. McCauley, you are such a snob!"

"A snob? I'm the most down-to-earth, easygoin' guy you'll ever meet."

"You denigrate everything that isn't Texan, for one thing. And you are absolutely convinced everyone else on the planet is inferior to those people you know personally."

He looked taken aback by her comments. Well, perhaps he'd never thought about his form of snobbery, but he should. No wonder he was still single when he was obviously heterosexual and definitely old enough to settle down.

Gwendolyn pitied the woman Hank finally married unless she was from Ranger Springs, Texas, and loved all things cowboy.

Someone like Kerry Lynn Jacks, no doubt. Although Hank hadn't seemed overly jealous of his former girlfriend running off with Prince Alexi, he might be hiding his true feelings. Perhaps Hank was still in love with the waitress.

The idea caused another emotion—this one more intense and less pleasant—to flutter inside Gwendolyn's chest. Jealousy. She didn't want to think of Hank and the waitress. She wanted to see him expand his horizons, change some of his rigid thinking and admit that "foreign" women could also have merit. British women, for example.

Oh, what nonsense! She had no business thinking of Hank in this manner. This was just another example of how confused and convoluted her thinking had become since Prince Alexi had run off and left her "high and dry," as Hank would say. She was half mad at herself and entirely peeved with Alexi when Hank spoke again.

"I'm no snob," he almost growled. "I just know who I am and what I like."

She whirled so she faced him. "Well, perhaps you could learn to like French wines, Russian caviar and handheld asparagus!"

He stepped closer, leaning forward in an intimidating male style she'd seen before. "I don't see why I should!"

Gwendolyn placed her hands on her hips to keep from curling them into fists and shaking them at Hank. "Maybe so no one mistakes you for a narrow-minded cowboy without any interests outside of the bedroom!"

"That's better than being recognized as a cold Brit with no interest *in* the bedroom."

"Oh, that's entirely unfair. You have no idea what interests I have!"

He leaned even closer, so close she could feel his hot breath on her face. "Oh, yeah? Why don't you tell me about them?"

"Ahem. Excuse me."

The sound of Milos Anatole's cultured voice cut through the tension like a knife. Gwendolyn jumped back; Hank straightened so abruptly she barely saw him move. Suddenly, three feet and some angry words stood between them.

"I'm sorry to interrupt your conversation, but we need to fit the tuxedo for tonight."

"That's quite all right. We were finished discussing that topic, anyway."

Hank muttered something that sounded like "the hell we were," but she couldn't be sure. Besides, she felt as though she'd been sparring with Lennox Lewis for at least three rounds.

"I have some correspondence to attend to while you continue with Mr. McCauley," she said, addressing Milos. "Please let me know if you need me for anything."

"Yes, Lady Gwendolyn. Come along, Mr. McCauley."

"I'm not a damned dog," he said peevishly. Despite her earlier anger, Gwendolyn found herself hiding yet another smile. He might be exasperating, but Hank McCauley could also be very entertaining, even to a "cold Brit."

HANK KNEW HE LOOKED LIKE a million bucks as he walked from the dining room in the back of the governor's mansion into the fancy double parlor. Everything looked very old, expensive and polished. He'd never anticipated dining with the governor and a couple of members of the U.S. House of Representatives, not to mention a half-dozen influential business and civic leaders. He'd never thought he'd be escorting such a beautiful, intelligent and cultured woman to anything resembling this fancy dinner.

Not the contessa. While she was beautiful, she didn't hold a candle to Lady Wendy. Tonight she was dressed in a simply cut dark blue satin gown with one of those draped necklines and an enticingly low back. Her bare skin was partially covered by some type of lace that swirled and beckoned for him to trace each curlicue. Not that he was going to give in to the urge. He just wished the damn dress didn't keep begging him to touch Gwendolyn's smooth, pale skin, especially when they were socializing in the Texas governor's mansion.

"Port, Your Highness?" the governor's wife asked as she beckoned a waiter over.

Hank smiled and nodded.

"I'm so sorry your voice is temporarily silent," their hostess continued. "I so love a foreign accent."

Hank smiled and looked down at Wendy, who was no doubt thinking the same thing about the Texas accent of most of the people attending tonight. It was probably a bad sign that he'd begun to sense what she was thinking, but he wasn't going to dwell on that right now, either.

He was going to try to relax, never forgetting he was Prince Alexi, and enjoy tonight's festivities. This might be his only opportunity to be in such exalted company.

"Excuse me," the first lady of Texas said. "I need to thank the congressman for making a special trip home from Washington." She walked toward the doorway to speak to a portly man who looked vaguely familiar.

Hank smiled and nodded while Gwendolyn stood beside him, silent but far from unnoticed.

The Contessa di Giovanni strolled over, her own escort a slightly built, dark Italian guy who looked like he should be selling shoes at Dillards. "Good evening, Your Highness," she said in her heavily accented English. Would the real prince enjoy listening to her husky voice for the next fifty years or so? He'd better, if his daddy was convinced this contessa would make a great princess. King Wilheim seemed like a real determined man—not to mention a powerful one.

"Contessa," Hank managed to rasp out as he'd been practicing. He placed a hand to his throat, wincing as though he were in pain.

"Your poor throat," the contessa purred as she placed a hand on his arm. "I am so sorry this happened on your trip abroad."

Hank nodded in sympathy.

"His Highness mentioned earlier today that he is equally sorry the two of you will not be able to converse, but he knows he will have other opportunities in the near future to speak to you privately."

The contessa beamed, which made her appear much

more appealing. At the same time, she looked a little calculating, so Hank wasn't entirely fooled into thinking she wanted ol' Alexi for his good looks and personality. A prince was a good catch for anyone, even someone who already had a title.

Hank wondered if Gwendolyn thought that way. Had she dreamed of marrying a prince when she was growing up in England? Of course, pickings were pretty slim in the British royal family. There was that one younger son, Edward—kind of nice-looking if you didn't mind his receding hairline—but he was finally married. To a public relations executive, no less.

"Contessa, would you and Mr. Previa join us?" their hostess asked, returning with a white-coated waiter who bore several small glasses of dark red port. Hank silently thanked Milos for his hours of instruction, which had included protocol on drinking and toasting.

Hank whispered in Wendy's ear. She listened, then nodded in approval. "His Highness, Prince Alexi, would like to make a toast to our gracious hostess for providing such a wonderful opportunity to meet Contessa di Giovanni."

Everyone raised his or her glass to the first lady of Texas while she smiled. Apparently he'd thought of the right thing to whisper, even if Wendy had put his sentiment in a little better wording. She sure did a good job making everyone feel special. Hank wondered if the real prince appreciated her, and if so, how much. Surely a woman like Wendy would make a darn fine princess. Heck, she already knew what to do and say in any situation. She and the prince would have some good-looking kids, too.

Hell, *he* and Wendy would have good-looking kids.

Oh, man, that thought had come out of left field. He had no business imagining little dark-haired, polite children with a mischievous glint in their blue eyes flecked with gold. He and Wendy were as different as...well, the contessa and that white-coated waiter. Red-blooded Texan and blue-blooded aristocrats didn't mix any better than chicken hawks and eagles.

"Prince Alexi?"

He turned to Wendy, who had placed a hand on his sleeve. Apparently he'd been daydreaming while the conversation had gone on around him.

He raised an eyebrow and took another sip of port. The fancy stuff was pretty good if you liked sweet wine. Real different from a good, cold beer.

The contessa asked in her heavily accented English, "I wondered if you will you be visiting the president at his ranch while you are here in Texas."

Hank frowned a little and shrugged.

"We haven't confirmed a visit yet. Events in Washington may keep the president away," Gwendolyn explained.

"What a shame," the contessa sighed. "Such a powerful man. I would *love* to meet him."

Hank kept from rolling his eyes by reminding himself that Alexi may end up marrying the Italian beauty with a lust for power. No doubt about it—she wanted to become a princess herself, then a queen. And who was he, a retired rodeo cowboy, to know if that's what was best for Belegovia? If Wendy thought the contessa was right for Alexi, Hank knew he had to play along.

He raised his glass and whispered hoarsely, "Splendid."

The contessa beamed. Wendy raised an eyebrow. "If you will excuse us, Contessa di Giovanni, Mr.

Previa, we need to speak to the secretary of state regarding some tourism opportunities.''

The two Italians nodded. Hank felt the contessa's calculating eyes on him as he walked with Wendy toward a group of men at the end of the room, standing beside a white marble fireplace.

Too bad he couldn't admit who he really was, he thought as he pretended to whisper intelligent conversation in Wendy's ear and she spoke to the powerful politicians. These men all had connections to the rich and famous, and many of them owned their own cutting horses. He could really use their influence to get his training facility off the ground. He'd planned to go to one of the futurity sales next month where he'd probably see some of these men or their representatives among the bidders. Would they comment on his likeness to the prince they'd had dinner and drinks with in Austin? He'd have to be on his guard to keep from slipping up.

Soon the drinks and talk came to an end. He managed to murmur ''marvelous evening'' to his host and hostess at the front door of the governor's mansion, accepting their warm goodbyes and hopes for a future relationship with Belegovia. Considering Texas was fives times as big and the economy was much, much larger in his home state than in the European country, he wondered what the two had in common. He'd have to ask Lady Wendy later.

With her nearly at his side—she always walked a step behind him while in public—he descended the steps and walked the short distance to the wrought-iron gates and waiting limo. They hadn't taken the Land Rover tonight, relying on an official Texas escort to and from the historic hotel where they were staying the night. Pete Boedecker had the night off, and Milos Anatole waited for them at the suite.

As soon as they were seated inside, Wendy reached across the darkness and squeezed his hand. He'd forgotten how tense she'd been about tonight, but at the moment, she seemed to be saying "good job." Or maybe "thank goodness that's over" was more like it. Too bad they couldn't talk in front of their driver, who worked for the State of Texas and wouldn't understand why Prince Alexi sounded like he'd lived all his life in the Hill Country rather than some fancy English estate.

They were whisked inside and entered the elevator before either of them could talk. A representative of the hotel accompanied them in the beautifully restored elevator, chatting about the history of the place, the other heads of state and movie stars who had stayed in the suite. Nodding good-night, Hank made it to his suite with a sigh of relief, only to discover Wendy wasn't beside him.

"Let me take your coat," Milos said, emerging quietly from the shadows. "I trust your evening went well?"

"Splendid," Hank said in his best Prince Alexi imitation. He wanted to talk to Wendy, unwind a bit before hitting the sack. He was glad to be finished playing his assigned role; now he wanted to be Hank McCauley for a while. Grab a beer from the little refrigerator in the fancy cabinet, prop his feet up on the coffee table in the sitting room and cruise through the channels on the television. He'd like to do all that with a certain English lady beside him.

Damn, he was getting too attached to her. He tried to tell himself it was the situation—being forced into close quarters with her most of the day—but he knew that wasn't all of what he was feeling. He'd grown to depend on her because he was Prince Alexi's stand-in, but as Hank McCauley he'd started to like her. Yeah, they were worlds apart, but she understood what he was going through better than anyone.

He had to fight the urge to share a little more of his life with her. Maybe admit he'd been a little more worried about pulling off this gig than he'd admitted, even to himself.

Before he could relax on his own, Milos had him out of the tux and into one of the hotel's thick terry-cloth robes. The valet excused himself to prepare the "prince's" wardrobe for the next day. Suddenly Hank was completely alone in the luxurious suite.

He did what he'd planned on earlier—grabbed a longneck and slouched on the fancy brocade sofa. He propped his bare feet on the cherry coffee table that was probably an antique and reached for his cell phone.

"Hey, Travis, it's Hank." For the next five minutes, he talked to his friend about the ranch, getting his daily update on his horses and phone calls from owners and buyers. Everything was going well, but he got a little homesick for the ranch he'd bought while he was still rodeoing.

After he finished the call, he surfed channels on the big television hidden inside a cherry armoire. He was a little disappointed that there wasn't a story on the prince's tour of Texas. He'd kind of wanted to see his picture on the television, posing as the prince. What a kick his friends at the feed store or the Four Square Café would get if they knew their ol' buddy was walking around in a designer tuxedo, shaking hands with the rich and powerful politicians in Austin.

He was about to flick off the television for the night when he heard a knock at the door. He unfolded his body from the couch and turned off the news channel. Padding across the soft, thick carpet on bare feet, he expected to see Milos Anatole on the other side, ready to give him more lessons on eating, drinking or greeting.

Instead, a fidgeting English lady waited in the hallway.

He opened the door, grinning widely. Damn, he was glad to see this woman. He said the first thing to come to his mind. "Time to learn how to eat barbecue with the president?"

Chapter Six

"No!" She brushed past him into the suite as he closed the door. "No, I just wanted to come by and tell you how much I appreciate what you've done. I was so worried about tonight, but you handled yourself admirably."

"I do my best to please," he said, slightly irritated that she didn't have more faith in his abilities to pull this off, even though he'd doubted himself from time to time.

"You were wonderful," she said, grasping her hands in front of her as she paced to the windows overlooking the street below. "Better than any of us hoped for."

"By golly, your faith in me is overwhelming."

Wendy spun around. "I didn't mean we lacked faith in you! You just far exceeded expectations."

"So do I get the employee-of-the-month pin and a special parking spot outside the palace?"

She walked to him, tilting her head in that inquisitive way of hers. "What?"

"Never mind. I was being sarcastic." She looked adorably rumpled, dressed in casual slacks and the T-shirt he'd bought for her in San Antonio. Her hair was loose and slightly tousled, as if she hadn't brushed it after pulling on the T-shirt.

He wanted to run his hands through the long, sleek strands. Tip her face up to his. Kiss her breathless…

"Please don't be," she said, placing her fingers on his sleeve. "You are an amazing man."

"Yeah?" he answered casually, trying not to think about how she stood within reach of his eager hands, trying to remember why getting naked with the English lady was a really bad idea.

"Absolutely."

He felt the atmosphere in the room thicken. The quiet. The darkness outside. The low light from a single lamp across the room. Him dressed in a robe and a pair of cotton briefs, which were getting tighter by the minute.

He took a deep breath as he turned away from Wendy's sincere expression. "How about something to drink? There's some white wine in the refrigerator, and some soft drinks."

"A glass of wine would be fine," she said as she walked around the couch and sat down. His half-finished beer was still on the coffee table, where he'd left it when he'd decided to go to bed. Alone.

Oh, boy. What was he getting himself into? The whole scene seemed too cozy for his peace of mind. Did she feel it, too? She must not, because surely she wouldn't put herself into a situation where he'd be tempted to forget their relationship was professional, not personal.

"Thank you," she said as he handed her the glass of chardonnay. "I hope I'm not keeping you up."

Not like you meant, he thought to himself. "No, I

was just unwinding. Believe it or not, I was a little concerned about tonight, too.''

Wendy—Lady Wendy to him—leaned closer. ''Oh, I know you must have been, but you certainly didn't show it.''

''After you've faced down a ton of ornery bull or twelve hundred pounds of angry horseflesh, you learn to keep your cool. The one thing you don't want to show them is fear.''

She shuddered. ''Your former profession sounds brutal.''

Hank shrugged. ''I loved it. My body got tired before my spirit got broken, so I guess I'm lucky.''

She took a sip of wine while her gaze checked him out. The robe did a good job of covering all the important things, which might shock her more than a few scars from bad breaks and surgery.

''So what about you, Lady Wendy? Did you always want to work for the prince?''

''No, I'd decided on a career in public relations when I was still at university. I joined a firm after school, but Alexi hired me away when he started traveling and promoting Belegovia a few years ago.''

''So you left England behind and started working for the prince.''

''Actually, I work for the royal family of Belegovia, but Prince Alexi is the spokesperson for the monarchy. He's done a wonderful job letting the world know of Belegovia's tourism and strong pro-American and pro-European culture.''

''Sounds like a good job. I guess your family is proud.''

The light in the room seemed to dim as Wendy looked away, frowning into her glass of wine. She placed it on the coffee table. "Not really. My father believed I should marry someone with a title and have two children, at least one of which must be a boy. He's rather keen on carrying on family names and titles. Since I did him no good in that department, I should marry and provide an heir for another peer."

"Yeah, a lot of guys are like that over here, too, only without those ancestral titles. In the States, it's more likely to be passing along the family business." Hank shrugged. "Of course, a lot of daughters take over when their daddies retire."

"It's a bit different when you're the eleventh earl of Epswich. Our family home was started in the fifteenth century, then added to by various ancestors. My father, however, and his father before him, don't have a true head for business."

"What does he do?"

"Do?" she questioned, shaking her head. "As little as possible, actually. He takes his seat in the House of Lords at least once a year, when he's not fox hunting or visiting his chums at their estates. Unfortunately, our estate doesn't support a stable of hunters or a kennel of hounds, so he relies on friends for his hobbies."

"I guess that's the definition of a country gentleman."

"I suppose, although I would have more respect for him if he'd spend more time managing our estate. My brother, the future Earl of Epswich—who, by the way, is an absolute ponce—is now hosting tours of our ancestral home."

Hank wondered if he was supposed to know what a ponce was. Instead, he focused on what he understood. "Tours? Like the gardens and the house?"

"Yes, and for approximately two hundred American dollars, tourists can sleep in one of the bedrooms with a shadowed history."

"What do you mean?"

Wendy twirled the stem of her glass between her fingers. "My brother may have exaggerated who slept where and when. I seriously doubt that Henry VIII ever honeymooned at Epswich Manor."

Hank laughed. "So Texans aren't the only ones who tell tall tales."

She smiled. "I'm surprised you'd admit such a thing."

"By the way, what is a ponce?"

"It means he's rather a smarmy toff."

Hank laughed. "Now who's talkin' in riddles."

Wendy laughed in return, raising her glass to her lips. "My brother and I aren't very close, but I shouldn't speak ill of him. Still, he's a bit pretentious and overbearing." She reached across the coffee table and handed him the longneck.

"It's late and you're tryin' to get me drunk," he said with a grin.

"I most certainly am not! You had already opened that beer when I arrived."

"So, maybe you're tryin' to seduce me," he teased, leaning closer. If he scared her off a little bit, she might get huffy and leave before he did something stupid. Like press her back into the cushions of this really nice couch, open his robe and shock her to the soles of her shoes.

"You are incorrigible."

"At least I'm not a ponce."

"No, you're not." Wendy settled back against the cushions, a genuine smile on her face. "You've made my job much easier after the prince put us in a difficult position.''

''I aim to please.'' He let his grin slip away as he looked into her eyes. ''What about you? What do you want to do next week, next year? Do you see yourself working for the prince for a long time?''

''I'm not sure. Probably. He's usually a very wonderful boss, and I truly like my job.''

''Really?'' Hank felt another stab of jealousy when he thought about Wendy's relationship with the prince. Did the guy appreciate what a great person she was? Didn't he find her attractive? He wanted to ask Alexi those questions, but then again, maybe he didn't want to know the answers.

''Don't you miss England?''

''Yes, but I visit several times a year. Since the prince grew up there, we return regularly.''

''How did that work, exactly? I'm not real good on European history.''

''When the Soviet Union took over countries in Eastern Europe after World War II, the Belegovian monarchs fled for their lives with just a few treasures they could carry. They sought asylum in England and it was granted. Truthfully, I believe King Wilheim believed he'd never see his homeland again. He was a teenager at the time.''

''So how old is the king now?''

''He's only sixty. I'm sure he'll be on the throne for many years.''

''So Alexi was actually born in England?''

''Yes. He and his brother and sister grew up knowing they were Belegovian royalty, but thinking and acting as good English citizens.''

"I guess it was tough going to a country they'd never seen."

"Yes, it was, but also an exciting challenge. Alexi does love a challenge."

"Which is probably what he's getting if he's off with Kerry Lynn."

Lady Wendy sat up on the couch, then started fidgeting with her hands. "I suppose the two of you were close, with both of you growing up in the same town."

Hank grinned. "Now, I told you there's no need for you to be jealous."

"Jealous! Of course I'm not jealous."

"Now, don't deny it. You made some comments before about Kerry Lynn, and I need to set the record straight. We dated for a while—maybe a month—but we decided we're really more friends than we are…lovers."

Wendy's eyes shot open. "Then you were—never mind."

"Close? Man, your eyes get really green when you're jealous."

"I am not jealous!" She shot off the couch like a big ol' spring had hit her in the butt. "I'm just trying to understand this relationship we seem to be involved in with Prince Alexi and your former girlfriend."

"Don't fib to me, Lady Wendy. You want down-and-dirty details."

"I most certainly do not!"

"Yeah, you do. You want to know if Kerry Lynn and I did the horizontal mambo. Then you'll want to know how it was for me. Before long, you'll be wondering if you and I would have a better time between the sheets."

"Of all the— You have no idea what you're talking about!"

He followed her over to the window. Her reflection in the darkened glass showed someone tormented by her own feelings, and he felt ashamed for teasing her so much. She was an English lady, not an easygoing Texan, and she didn't understand how red-blooded American males thrived on testing and challenging a woman they were interested in.

He placed his hands on her shoulders. She jumped, and he made a soothing sound close to her ear. "I'm sorry, Lady Wendy. I was just teasin' you."

"You have no idea how much pressure I'm under. King Wilhelm called again earlier and I had to tell him you couldn't talk to him because of your laryngitis. I'm sure he wanted to discuss both this trip and his plans for Prince Alexi to marry soon. The king wasn't happy."

"I know you did a good job smoothing over those waters."

"I tried, but sometimes I…"

"What?" he asked, massaging her shoulders.

She sighed and began to relax under his hands. "Sometimes I'd like to shake Alexi until his eyeballs rattled. I'd like to yell at him and tell him to quit running off. I know he believes some of these events I schedule aren't important—at least not important to him—but that's my job! He's always been this way, taking a short holiday when he's under stress, but he's bloody well grown now."

Hank nodded. "You're right. Let's go find the bounder and hang him by his thumbs."

Wendy smiled at him in the window's reflection. "If it were only that easy. He's not answering his mobile phone. If he doesn't want to be found, I'm afraid that we can't search without letting on he's missing.''

"You forgot one thing," he said, turning her around. "He's with Kerry Lynn. There's no way in hell she'd miss her college graduation ceremony on Saturday in San Marcus. She's worked too hard for that degree in business, waiting tables and helping her mother and sisters get by. She'll be there if she has to hog-tie and gag that prince.''

"So you believe he'll show up on Saturday? Or maybe tomorrow?''

The hopeful look in her eyes made Hank smile. "I'm sure of it.''

She grasped his arms. "I hope you're right. I genuinely need to shake some sense into him.''

Hank grinned. "I'd like to see that." But he didn't want to talk about Kerry Lynn or Alexi or anything else at the moment. Leaning down, he kept watching Wendy as he parted his lips, letting her know exactly what he was thinking. Exactly what he was going to do—even though he knew it was pure foolishness.

Her eyes widened and her hands tightened on his arms. "Close your eyes, darlin'," he whispered before he covered her lips with his.

Unlike the other quick, unexpected kisses, this one was sweet and slow. He teased her wide, expressive mouth, coaxing her lips apart. His tongue traced the curve, entered slightly, retreated and pressed home. Glorious. That's what kissing this English lady felt like. She tasted crisp and sweet, just like the wine she'd sipped. She melted against him and he pulled her tight.

He wanted to part the thick terry robe and hold her close to his hot body. He wanted her to feel how he'd gone from on-alert to full attention in two seconds flat, but that might frighten her. For all her worldly experience—living in England and Belegovia, hobnobbing with the rich and famous—she was surprisingly hesitant. Kind of…innocent.

She pulled away with a gasp. Hank looked down into her wide eyes, then noticed her heaving chest. He was a little surprised to discover his own breathing wasn't so steady, either.

"This is not a good idea," she whispered. "Things are complicated enough without…this."

"It was just a kiss," he said gently, smoothing his fingers through her silky hair. "Don't make more of it than we need to."

"But—"

He placed a finger on her lips. Her soft, hot, slightly damp lips. "Sure enough, that kiss could be the beginning of a great night if you wanted it to be, but it doesn't have to be."

"I don't want you to think—"

"Darlin', I've been thinkin' those thoughts about you for quite a while. That doesn't mean I have to act on them—unless you want me to."

She just looked at him, not saying a thing. Not denying her feelings, that was for sure. He almost took advantage of her uncertainty before he remembered she was scared. Scared that she'd mess up this trip, scared that the prince wasn't going to show up with Kerry Lynn on Saturday.

"I tell you what. Why don't we go find that runaway prince?"

"Do you truly think we could?"

"I know just about everyone from Austin to San Antone. If Kerry Lynn and the prince are still together, we'll find them. Texas is a big state, but Ranger Springs is a tight-knit community.''

"Finding Prince Alexi would solve my problems.''

Hank didn't want to think about what that meant for him. She wouldn't need him any longer. She'd go on with the prince's tour and he'd go back to his ranch.

She frowned. "But if you're not impersonating the prince any longer, why would you continue to help me?''

"Because, Lady Wendy, I *did* agree to help you. I wouldn't be a credit to Texas or the legacy of cowboys in general if I let a lady in distress go off on her own, now, would I?''

"I suppose not.''

"Of course not. So we're in this together until that wayward prince shows up.''

She smiled. "You are truly a prince, Hank McCauley.''

"Naw, I'm just a regular guy.''

Finally, her face reflected hope. "I could send out a press release that your symptoms have worsened into a potentially infectious—''

"Darlin', why don't you just tell them I have a cold.''

"Yes, a cold is good. And you need to cancel the rest of your appearances in Texas to recover, especially since I just learned that the president won't be at his ranch this weekend.''

"Right. And we'll head back to Ranger Springs to search for Kerry Lynn and lover boy.''

"Good plan,'' she said, her eyes lighting up with excitement. "I'll write the press release immediately.''

"You sure this won't cause any of that rabid speculation by the tabloids?''

She shook her head. "I don't believe so, not when you made appearances with laryngitis."

His grip on her arms stopped her. "One thing before you rush off to deceive the public again." He gave her one of his slow, sexy smiles, then waited for her reaction. He wasn't disappointed; she melted just a bit before he continued. "Kerry Lynn and I never did set the sheets on fire. We had a good time, had a lot in common, but the spark just wasn't there."

"Spark?"

He grinned. "Yeah, the spark. You know what I mean. It's that feelin' you and I get when we look at each other."

"We do not…spark." She stiffened, as if she'd just remembered she was supposed to be arguing with him, not kissing him until he couldn't think straight.

"Oh, yeah we do, Lady Wendy. You might as well go ahead and admit it now, because those little sparks can turn into a full-out blaze if you're not careful."

OF ALL THE IRRESPONSIBLE actions she might have taken, kissing Hank McCauley in his hotel suite was right at the top of the list. If she were totally honest, using the flimsy excuse of thanking him for his "performance" at the governor's mansion was even more daft. If she hadn't put herself in such a situation, she wouldn't have been tempted by his fantastic body and enticing lips. Not to mention his sexy smile and bedroom eyes.

She groaned as she secured the locks on her hotel room door and sagged against the wall. She had to remember her goal—find the prince and ensure no one learned of the deception. Placate King Wilheim and chastise Prince Alexi, then return to Belegovia and forget about Hank McCauley.

Her life was that simple; there was no other choice. She refused to admit defeat. She would not return to England and explain to her family—especially her father—that she'd failed in her first opportunity to distinguish herself from the thousands of other public relations persons who aspired to work for the royals.

Her career remained the most important part of her life at the moment. She was only twenty-nine years old; plenty of time remained before she started hearing the loud ticking of her biological clock. Besides, she'd yet to meet a man who made her want to settle for nappies and formula rather than business suits and a career. Her few attempts at a serious relationship proved failures when she'd expected her partner to be monogamous and understanding. Geoffrey had told her that if her job came first, he needed to seek companionship elsewhere while she was "busy." She'd learned from Carlos that a man's career came first; she needed to accommodate her schedule to his far more important assignments.

Gwendolyn was reminded of a clever sign she'd read in a restaurant: a woman needs a man like a fish needs a bicycle. She understood completely that she *didn't* need a man to make her complete.

But oh, she truly wanted Hank McCauley to send sparks flying. Although he wasn't the happily-ever-after type of man that she'd been raised to admire, he was the devil-may-care type of lover that she'd fantasized about for years.

He was also absolutely off limits to her fantasies, her thoughts, and especially any part of her body.

Unfortunately, her wayward lips didn't want to lis-

ten to such a logical argument. Her lips wanted her to
march right back to the presidential suite, grab the
lapels of that thick robe and pull him close for another
heart-stopping kiss.

''No!'' she said aloud as she marched into the bathroom. She was going to finish her nightly routine,
moisturizing her skin so she didn't become sunburned
and parched from the Texas sun. She was going to
brush and floss her teeth so she didn't have to endure
any of Hank's ridiculous jests about English dental
health. And she was going to forget her inappropriate
fascination with one infuriating Texas cowboy.

TRAVIS LEANED BACK AGAINST the bar and took a sip
of his draft beer, wondering what Hank was up to at
the moment. Had the woman been worth the trip out
of town? Hank took his ranch seriously, so she must
be something special.

Under normal conditions, he wouldn't miss the go-
ing-away party for one of Ethan Parker's officers, Rick
Alvarado. The festivities were in full swing at
Schultze's Roadhouse. They'd reserved the back
room, but the party had spilled over into the main part
of the bar, and now everyone was mingling with the
locals who'd come in for a few beers and some barbecue.

Of course, the fact that most of the Ranger Springs
Police Department was in attendance put a damper on
serious drinking.

''So, where's Hank tonight? I thought for sure he'd
be here,'' Susie O'Donald, Ethan's daytime dispatcher, asked as she joined him at the bar.

''He had to go out of town for a few days. I'm sure
he's real sorry he missed the party.''

"I have a couple of girlfriends who wish he'd shown up," Susie teased. "Of course, they'd settle for a dance with you."

"Gee, don't flatter me so much. My head will swell."

Susie laughed. "I'm just teasing, although you have to admit Hank is a good-looking devil."

"He's not my type," Travis said, looking down at the cute, very married dispatcher who loved to get involved in local gossip as much as the two veterans, Thelma and Joyce, down at the Four Square Café.

"Well, come on over and dance with Gina Mae Summers," Susie said, grasping his arm. "She's turned down Tug Hanson and Lester Boggs, but they're bound to come back."

"You know I'm not much of a dancer."

"That's why we miss Hank so much. But you'll do in a pinch," Susie replied as she pulled him across the floor. "You're better than Lester or Tug."

"Faint praise," he replied as they neared the booth where Gina, the cute red-haired real estate agent sat with Robin Parker. "Hi there, ladies."

"Hank's not here?" Robin asked.

Travis moaned. He sure wished his friend would drag his sorry butt away from whatever lady had captured his attention. The ladies of Ranger Springs— even the married ones—needed him here.

Chapter Seven

Gwendolyn's second trip to Hank McCauley's ranch gave her an entirely different perspective from the first trip. For one thing, they traveled in his huge pickup truck, the "dually" with surprising luxuries she hadn't truly appreciated when she'd first ridden in the vehicle. She settled back into the leather bucket seat and watched the Texas landscape rush by through a dark tinted window, a blast of air-conditioning a welcome relief from the hot weather outside. There was a bench seat behind them in the "extended cab," as Hank had explained the configuration, for guests or workers. And there were all sorts of gadgets and technical marvels not usually found in European cars.

Outside, the landscape of rolling hills and winding roads beckoned her attention. Wildflowers bloomed everywhere, alongside the two- and four-lane highways, struggling through rocky outcroppings and peeking around weathered fence posts. Short bushy cactus and yucca plants contributed to a scene that was both foreign and fascinating to someone who had grown up among rain-drenched English gardens, towering trees and cultivated hedgerows.

"We'll be at the ranch in about fifteen minutes,"

Hank said, breaking into her thoughts. "If you need anything, we can stop at the Kash 'n' Karry."

"I'm fine." She was already the proud owner of a new pair of form-fitting jeans, a western-cut shirt that placed undo emphasis on her breasts, and a baseball-style cap that proclaimed a love of Texas with a big red embroidered heart over an outline of the state. Hank had delivered the items to her room early this morning, telling her to put her hair into a ponytail, wear some glossy lipstick and try to look like a Texan when they walked out of the hotel.

Apparently she needed a disguise now that Hank had returned to his persona. Seeing Prince Alexi's public relations coordinator with a Texas cowboy who looked just like the prince would raise too many questions now that the paparazzi had caught up with them.

Milos Anatole now occupied the prince's suite, pretending to have a cold and laryngitis whenever the phone rang. He did a much more credible imitation of Prince Alexi's voice than Hank ever could. Gwendolyn wished she'd thought of using him for that function earlier. The valet had proved invaluable for many reasons. She'd need to talk to Alexi about giving him a bonus for his service.

When she found Alexi. If she was still speaking to him after this last fiasco. Running away from his life wasn't the answer to whatever was bothering him.

"Penny for your thoughts, Lady Wendy."

Startled to hear Hank's voice, she shook her head. Only then did she realize she'd been frowning. "I was thinking of Prince Alexi. Where he is right now, what he's doing, how I'm going to murder him when he reappears."

Hank chuckled. "I'm sure he's shakin' in his Italian loafers."

Wendy looked away from the gently rolling hills to focus on Hank. "If I know Alexi, he's dressed in disreputable jeans, a ratty old Harvard T-shirt and some battered athletic shoes. He's probably drinking beer and doing other manly things he's rarely allowed in Belegovia."

"Really? Well, my respect for the guy just went up a notch." He frowned. "Except for that Harvard shirt. The University of Texas would be a lot better choice, especially if he's running around the Lone Star State."

"He's rather fond of his alma mater."

"I can understand that."

"Does that mean you went to the University of Texas?" She tried to keep the skepticism out of her voice—she'd always heard that professional athletes weren't keen on education—but she wasn't sure she'd been successful.

He must have seen through her because he grinned. "I actually graduated, too, although it took me a long time. I left college to rodeo full-time when I was twenty, but I'd always promised my momma that I'd finish, so when I got injured I kept my word."

Her respect for Hank McCauley increased. Anyone who kept his word to his mother deserved admiration.

Gwendolyn had tried to keep her pledge to her mother, who had passed away nearly fifteen years ago. All her mother wanted was for the family to stay close, to work together to make a success of Epswich Manor.

Some promises were easier to keep than others.

She wished Alexi could accept what she'd learned through her difficult relationship with her father and siblings: personal and professional success was the best defense against the censure of one's relatives. Alexi needed to discover how to reconcile his need for independence with his father's need for control.

He especially needed to face the problem of finding a princess everyone agreed upon. Truly, with all the women in Europe who were vying for his affections, surely he could find one that he liked well enough to court.

"When do you think we can look for Prince Alexi?" she asked.

"I'll make some phone calls as soon as we get settled at the ranch. If he and Kerry Lynn are around, I'll be able to find them."

"How can you be so sure?"

"Mrs. Jacks lives here and works at the Four Square Café. I can find out, like I said before, which relatives Kerry Lynn was visiting and start there. Besides, there aren't many secrets in a small town," Hank said with another grin. "Especially in Ranger Springs."

"I hope you're right. The longer the prince is gone, the stronger my urge to shake him grows."

Hank laughed. "He really ticked you off. I'm surprised. When you first showed up at the ranch a few days ago, you didn't seem all that angry."

"Looks can be deceiving…as I'm sure you can appreciate."

"You're right. Who would have thought you could have made a silk purse out of a sow's ear like me?"

"Oh, that's not what I meant at all! Please, don't compare yourself to a pig's ear." He was much more than some raw material that needed to be processed into something else. He'd taken the role seriously, learning when he'd seemed to be loafing, applying himself so effortlessly that she hadn't realized how hard he was trying.

"Thanks. I've learned a lot about wining and dining with the rich and famous."

A suspicion popped into her head. Suddenly, Hank's involvement in her dilemma made sense. "Was that why you really agreed to help me? So you could learn etiquette and protocol?"

Hank shrugged as he pulled onto his property. "Seemed like a good idea."

"But why?"

"The people who can afford quality cutting horses have a lot of money. Some of them are just good ol' boys like me, but a lot of them are athletes, movie stars and businessmen who want an exciting hobby."

"I see." He wanted to know how to mingle with his potential clients. How very clever of him to use her proposal for such a purpose.

He slowed over a rutted section of road and gave her a heart-stopping grin. "You're a damned good teacher."

"Milos did most of the instruction."

"Then you're a damned fine inspiration."

She sat back in the leather seat and permitted a genuine smile. Sometimes cowboys gave the nicest compliments.

HE'D NEVER SEEN ANYONE less adept at ranch living than Lady Wendy, although she did give it a good British try. The problem was that she wanted everything to be neat, orderly and immediate. Unfortunately, horses, weather and cowboys weren't influenced much by the need of an English aristocrat to get them organized.

He leaned back against the fence and smiled as she picked her way across the clumpy grass that separated the house from the barn. As yards went, it wasn't much to look at, but the grass would be dry and brown by the end of June, anyway, so nobody bothered with mowing or fertilizing.

She was still wearing the clothes he'd bought for her just that morning in Austin, although she'd taken off her baseball cap once they'd gotten into the truck. Except for the way she was walking across the yard— as if she was going to trip and fall flat on her face— she looked damned fine in those jeans and the body-hugging shirt.

He'd like to see her really relax like she'd done that night in San Antonio when he'd filled her up with tequila sunrises. He'd bet those nice curvy hips of hers would look real good if she'd just let herself go with the flow. Right now she looked more like a determined little tugboat than a fine sailing vessel.

"We need to make those phone calls," she said as she stopped in front of him and shaded her eyes against the midday sun.

"What you need is a real hat, Lady Wendy, not that little cap I got for you in Austin. I'm gonna look for one around the house and tack room."

"Very well, but I'd like to find Prince Alexi before nightfall, if possible. He's still not answering his mobile."

"As soon as I go into the house, I'll look up Kerry Lynn's momma's number."

"Can you do it now?"

"I really need to see this horse." He'd talked to his friend Travis about the new arrival and wanted to see the horse for himself.

"Surely the prince is more important than a horse."

"Whoa, now. You're the one who lost the prince. I've still got a ranch to run, and this horse arrived for training while we were runnin' around Austin with the rich folks and politicians. I need to see to him first."

She took in a deep breath as though she was going to blast him for his attitude, but apparently thought better of it. She let out her breath slowly. "I thought we were in agreement about the need to find the prince now."

"Absolutely. And as soon as I see this horse move, I'll get my butt right inside the house and call Mrs. Jacks."

He could tell Lady Wendy wasn't happy by her tight lips and stiff posture. Fortunately, she didn't say another word as Hank transferred his attention to the man who was closing the gate.

"Let him go, Juan," Hank shouted across the big pen.

A flashy bay gelding lunged forward as soon as the lead rope was unfastened, his black mane and tail rippling with every move. Hank wasn't sure if the horse could work cattle, but he sure had style. His burnished brown coat had red highlights just like this English lady's hair—not that she'd appreciate being compared to a horse.

"Oh, he's beautiful," Lady Wendy sighed as she grasped the fence and watched the gelding circle in a bouncing trot.

"He is that. Now we need to see if he has cow sense and intelligence."

"How will you do that?"

"You expect me to tell you all my secrets, Lady Wendy? Why, you might just take my trainin' techniques back to Merry Old England and make those fox hunters into cuttin' horses. Then your daddy and his friends would be roundin' up cows instead of pickin' on those poor little foxes.''

Hank watched her smile, then laugh, at the mental image of English gentlemen herding cattle. She didn't laugh nearly often enough. The joy transformed her face, making her appear much more the woman and less the bossy, cool and efficient managerial type. Not that she wasn't really good at her job. Heck, she could probably run his ranch—administratively, at least— with one arm tied behind her back. He admired that in a person. But at the moment, he was more interested in her as a woman.

That bothered him. He kept forgetting they didn't have a relationship outside this prince fiasco. As soon as Lady Wendy didn't need him any longer, she'd be gone faster than he could say ''scoot.''

But for now, she needed him...

''Let him run a little and unwind, Juan. We'll start working with him tomorrow.'' Hank turned away from the new bay gelding and Lady Wendy's genuine smiles. She was right; he needed to get to work on *her* problem so both of them could get on with their real lives.

He glanced at his watch. Mrs. Jacks was probably still working since it wasn't two o'clock yet. The Four Square Café had a weekday lunch crowd that didn't dwindle away until after one o'clock, especially on a Friday.

Instead of calling around, he decided to take a trip into town to find Kerry Lynn's mother. Besides, as much as he enjoyed being back home after two days away, he needed to put a little space between himself and Wendy.

Maybe he should quit calling her by that nickname. Thinking of her as Lady Gwendolyn Reed would be a lot safer than teasing her about her British roots.

She followed him across the dusty yard as he walked toward the house. "I've decided I'm goin' into town to talk to Kerry Lynn's momma," he said before his guest asked.

"I'll come with you. I need to check into a hotel, anyway."

He stopped walking. "That's not a good idea."

"Whyever not? I need to speak to the prince as quickly as possible, and I haven't procured a room for the night."

"For one thing, nobody in town knows you, which means everybody is gonna ask questions. Now, if they hear you talk they'll know you're not from around here."

"Yes, well, I won't talk to anyone."

Hank chuckled. "You obviously don't know small Texas towns. Before you knew what hit you, Thelma would have interviewed you for the newspaper and Joyce would have booked you for a hair appointment. Gina Mae Summers would see if you were interested in a house, and Chief Parker would have your life history, just in case you were plannin' to rob the bank or somethin' else illegal."

"They sound very...colorful."

They're just good folks, but the point is you can't waltz into town and ignore the locals." He grinned. "Besides, you'd be with me, which means everyone would want to know your name, where you're from and what you do for a livin' just so they could decide if you were good enough for one of their own.''

''I see.'' She sighed, shading her eyes with her hand as she looked up at him with wide, whisky-colored eyes. Not only did she need a hat, he reminded himself, but also sunscreen. Her pale English complexion would shrivel up in the harsh Texas sun.

''You'll give me a report as soon as possible?'' she asked.

''I'll let you know as soon as I find out where those two runaway lovebirds are holed up.''

''But what about the hotel?''

''Darlin', you're gonna be stayin' at this ranch.''

''I can't possibly!''

''I don't see why not. I have a perfectly good guest bedroom. Besides, I insist you accept my Texas hospitality. Ranger Springs,'' he said with a wink, ''doesn't have a hotel.''

THE FOUR SQUARE CAFÉ regulars had gone for the day except for Pastor Carl Schleipinger, who was sipping a cup of coffee while he read one of his religious magazines. He looked up as the bell over the door tinkled a welcome. A crumb-littered plate that looked as if it had once held cherry pie sat on the gray Formica table. Hank greeted the minister as he passed his table, then made his way to the back.

At the rear red vinyl booth, Mrs. Jacks and the other waitress were rolling knives, forks and spoons into paper napkins for the next meal. Hank grinned as he thought of the fancy dinner he'd attended just last night. There must have been a dozen different pieces of silverware at each place setting along the linen-draped table, which had sat at least twenty people.

No paper napkins for that crowd.

"Hello, ladies."

"Why, hi there, Hank. How are you?" Mrs. Jacks said. "Are you looking for Kerry Lynn?"

"Yes, ma'am, I sure am. Have you seen her lately?"

"I talked to her just this morning."

"Do you have a few minutes?"

Mrs. Jacks looked at the other waitress, a young woman with overprocessed hair and blue eye shadow, then up at him. "Why, it's been ages since we've had a chance to talk. I think I'll take my break now so we can visit." She looked at her fellow worker. "You don't mind, do you Clarice?"

"Not at all. We're almost finished here, anyway."

Mrs. Jacks worked her way out of the booth. Hank stepped back to give her room, then followed her through the swinging door to the kitchen. The smells of burgers, fries and other luncheon favorites hung in the air, although the grill had been cleaned and the fryers stood empty.

The small office was vacant, and Mrs. Jacks pulled out the two chairs in front of the metal desk. "Have a seat, Hank, and let me tell you what I know."

"I'm real concerned about Kerry. Do you know who she's with?"

Mrs. Jacks looked around as if someone might be eavesdropping, twisting her hands as she'd been turning the napkins around the silverware. "Well...do you?"

"Yeah, I do."

"That prince," Mrs. Jacks whispered. "The one who looks like you. They're in Galveston."

Hank nodded.

"I just couldn't believe it when she told me. I mean, a prince! And then I started wondering if he was one of those European playboys, and I just about went after them in my Buick."

"The prince's people say he's a good guy." Hank wasn't going to make any personal claims, since he'd never met the man, but Lady Wendy did think highly of him—when she didn't want to shake or strangle him.

"Oh, I hope so. I trust Kerry Lynn, of course, but I just can't believe she took a perfect stranger with her to Galveston. And why in the world would a prince want to go to the Texas coast in an old un-air-conditioned Toyota?"

Hank shrugged. He had no idea what had prompted the prince's desertion of his duties, except that Kerry Lynn was as cute as a bug. "What's she doin' in Galveston?"

"My brother and his wife, who live in Galveston, had a really nice little car they didn't need anymore after her mother went into the retirement home. We took up a collection in the family and bought it for a real good price as a graduation present for Kerry."

"So she went down to get the car."

Mrs. Jacks nodded. "With Prince Alexi," she whispered, just in case anyone was lurking.

"We've been lookin' for the prince for the past couple of days."

"You mentioned the prince's people. Who are they?"

"Lady Wendy Reed and his valet, Milos, mostly. They kind of…asked me to help them out."

"I know. Why are *you* looking for him?"

"Because he ran off in the middle of his big Texas

tour, leavin' his poor public relations director with all these engagements and no prince! So she asked me to fill in until we could find him.''

''And this has been going on since the day Kerry left?''

''That's right.''

''I saw that TV news report from the station in San Antonio of the prince visiting kids at the hospital.''

Hank grinned. He wished he'd seen himself on TV in Austin. ''Cute little kids, except the ones who were really sick. That just about broke my heart, but I kept on smilin'. Wendy is real big on keepin' up a good front.''

''Is Wendy the public relations person? The English lady?''

''Yeah, her real name's Lady Gwendolyn Reed, and she's sharp as a tack, too. Keeps me on a short leash.'' He thought back to the several times he'd talked her into stopping their sessions, how he'd kissed her, how he kept thinking about doing a lot more. ''Well, at least she tries to keep me under control.''

Mrs. Jacks reached over and patted his hand. ''I know what you mean, dear. You always were convincing when you wanted your way.''

Hank grinned. ''Thanks, Mrs. Jacks.''

''That wasn't necessarily a compliment, Hank.''

He decided to ignore that comment. ''So, where was Kerry when she called you?''

''They were leaving Galveston. She said they might take the long way around, to show the prince a little more of Texas.''

''Tell me, did she mention anything about the prince being in disguise? I mean, if I'm pretending to be him, who's he pretending to be?''

"Well...I think he's dressed in jeans." Mrs. Jacks rubbed her chin, then her eyes lit in amusement. "I imagine he looks a lot like...you."

"I see." So not only had Alexi stolen Hank's former girlfriend, now he'd taken his identity as well. Could this get any more complicated? "Any idea what time she'll get into town on Saturday?"

"No, I'm sorry, but she couldn't say. I think they're mostly sightseeing." Mrs. Jacks frowned. "At least, I hope that's what they're doing."

"So now she's a tour guide," Hank grumbled, shaking his head. "That European playboy is gonna make her late for her graduation, but I don't suppose he can be too bothered by things like that, seein' how he wants to take the long way back."

"I'm sure they'll be in San Marcus in time for her ceremony. The girls and I are driving over just after lunch tomorrow."

"Will you call me at the ranch if...*when* you hear from Kerry? I really need to get that prince to call Lady Wendy."

"I'll do my best."

Hank left out the back of the Four Square Café, vague discomfort growing like a bad case of black mold. He didn't like the idea that someone was running around pretending to be him. He didn't like the fact that Mrs. Jacks had to keep this a secret, just like he did. He couldn't share a laugh about this with his friends at Schultze's Roadhouse, at least not until everything was settled. Hell, Lady Wendy probably wouldn't want him to talk about it ever. Keeping secrets just wasn't in his nature.

The town he'd known all his life suddenly seemed to be pressing in around him as he stood in the narrow alley between the café and an old furniture store that had closed years ago. He even felt as though someone might be watching him as he pulled his hat lower on his forehead and walked quickly toward the truck.

He stopped when he got to the dually, looking up at the two-story buildings that surrounded the town square. The aged weathered brick walls and limestone cornerstones looked like old friends, but the blank, darkened windows on the second floor appeared more like searching eyes.

But nobody was looking down on him from those windows, just like no one knew he'd been pretending to be the prince for two days. He was probably just feeling guilty about all this deception. He prided himself on being a straight-up kind of guy, so fooling his friends and neighbors didn't settle well even if there was a good reason.

He unlocked the dually and slipped inside. As soon as the prince came back, things would return to normal, he told himself as he cranked the engine.

Lady Wendy would return to her life in Europe.

Well, of course she would. She was damned good at her job and didn't have any reason to stay a day longer than scheduled in Texas. She probably had the prince's life all planned out for the next year. With the king picking out the bride and Lady Wendy coordinating everything else, Prince Alexi would find himself married before he could say "goodbye, carefree bachelor."

Not that the lives of any of those people should matter to him, Hank reminded himself as he pulled out of the parking space. Hell, he'd never even met Prince Alexi or King Wilheim, and he'd only known Lady Wendy for three days. She'd marched in and disrupted his life; he should be glad when things got back to normal.

Except he had a strong suspicion that he'd kind of miss the bossy English lady.

Hank shook his head. He was thinking too much, that's all, letting his imagination get out of control. After only two days of playing the prince, he'd gotten accustomed to people watching him. Now he felt as though they were even when he was just plain ol' Hank McCauley, driving his pickup home from a nice, simple meeting with his ex-girlfriend's mother.

He flipped on the radio and listened to Clint Black sing about love as the familiar scenery streamed by. He hadn't listened to much country-and-western music since the Riverwalk on Wednesday night and it had affected his mood. He hadn't been on the back of a horse or brewed any oil-sludge coffee, and he'd missed that, too. Maybe his life wasn't all that exciting to European aristocrats, but he liked it just fine, he told himself.

Before long he pulled up beside the house and cut the engine. He wondered what Wendy had been up to while he was gone. Coming up with excuses why she couldn't stay at the ranch, most likely. He chuckled and shook his head as he walked toward the back door.

"Honey, I'm home," he called out as he removed his hat and tossed it on the kitchen table.

Chapter Eight

Gwendolyn felt like the proverbial curious cat as she wandered the rooms of Hank's house. Other than needing a good cleaning, it was well maintained. When she'd first seen the structure, she'd assumed it was an older home. In England, one simply didn't see this type of construction, with wooden planks, limestone accents and fireplaces, and a metal roof that looked almost antique. But now she realized that this was a fairly new house, with certain modern conveniences that one wouldn't have found early in the twentieth century.

Hank had a well-outfitted office with a state-of-the-art computer, laser printer and fax machine. At least she'd be able to send press releases and communicate with the media, whether Alexi showed up or not.

The bathrooms were especially nice, with a slightly dusty but otherwise clean guest bath complete with folded towels and tiny shell-shaped soaps. Gwendolyn wondered who had chosen the small amenities...and why. Perhaps an old girlfriend? Perhaps the elusive Kerry Lynn herself?

A spike of unwelcome jealousy stopped Gwendolyn cold. She absolutely must quell these ridiculous feelings of ownership of Hank McCauley. He was not *her* cowboy! He was an employee—albeit one who had yet to name his price, which worried her whenever she let herself think about it—and she needed to remember their relationship.

But, oh, it was difficult when she thought of the kisses they'd shared. When she remembered how wonderful he'd felt as he'd pressed his body close to hers. He was bigger than life in every way, and she longed to absorb some of his energy and heat for the long months ahead, when she'd try to forget about him.

Which would be difficult to do since Prince Alexi would remind her of Hank from now until eternity.

She wandered into the doorway of his bedroom, the darkened interior showing little of the man who slept there. The bed was unmade, a dark fluffy comforter half on and half off the king-size mattress. Two windows flanked the bed, revealing nightstands with the bare minimum—a lamp and what appeared to be a clock radio. No frilly woman's touch marred the simplicity, but she wondered if he had many visitors to this bachelor's domain. Overnight visitors who left a trail of lingerie on the way to that big bed…

"Honey, I'm home."

She heard his greeting, surprised she hadn't noticed his huge pickup truck returning to the ranch, or even the door opening and closing. With a flush spreading over her cheeks, she hurried down the hall, hoping he wouldn't catch her snooping around his personal space.

She wasn't so lucky.

"See anything interestin', Lady Wendy?"

His tone was teasing, but she bristled just the same.

"I took my suitcase into the guest room and I was just getting my bearings when—"

"Good. You found out where my bedroom is. That way, if you decide to sleepwalk, you'll know right where to come."

"I most certainly do not sleepwalk!"

Hank shook his head. "Too bad."

He was teasing her again, but she wasn't going to fall for his Texas charm. She tried to walk around him, but he spread his arms against the walls, blocking her in the hallway. "I'd like to continue with my unpacking, please."

"Aren't you gonna ask me about the prince?"

She stiffened. While she should have been worried about her job, she'd been thinking of Hank's bedroom activities. What was it about this man that kept her so unsettled?

"Yes! Did you discover his current whereabouts?"

"Not exactly. Why don't we take a seat in the livin' room and relax. I'll tell you what I found out from Mrs. Jacks."

"Of course." She once again tried to get by him, but he didn't move.

"Unless you'd like a better look at my bedroom," he said in a husky voice that promised more than "looking."

"Truly, I was just orienting myself in your house, which is very nice, by the way. Now that I know where the rooms are located, I can function much better."

"Function, hmm?" he remarked, reaching for a strand of her hair and twisting it around his finger. "I certainly want you to be comfortable while you're here."

"I'm sure I'll be fine. I'm also sure Alexi will return and I won't be here long."

Hank dropped her hair as though it had scorched him. "I guess you're right," he said, dropping his other hand from the wall and straightening. "I'm gonna get a beer. You want anything to drink?"

"A soft drink, perhaps."

"Fine."

He sounded slightly miffed as he turned and walked toward the kitchen. What had she said? Surely he didn't want her to stay any longer than necessary. He'd made it clear she was disrupting his life; he certainly didn't want a fussy English lady invading his private life for any longer than necessary.

She didn't understand Hank McCauley, even though she'd always thought of herself as someone who grasped the male psyche fairly well. Her father and brother certainly weren't a mystery, and her few serious boyfriends hadn't been complicated. Alexi... well, he was different. Complex and intelligent, he also had issues related to his royal family assuming the throne of Belegovia. But even Alexi wasn't as difficult to read as this Texas cowboy.

She perched on the edge of a couch that looked much older than the house. Hank returned shortly with a bottle of beer and a glass of a soft drink over ice. "I sure hope you like Dr. Pepper, 'cause that's all I have in the house."

"I've never tasted it, but I'm sure it's fine." She took a sip and tried not to show her surprise. The dark liquid was as different from a cola as Hank was from Alexi.

"What did you learn?"

He looked at her blankly.

"About Alexi's whereabouts? While you were in town?"

He relaxed back into a leather recliner. "I talked to Kerry's momma at the Four Square Café. She'd talked to Kerry just this morning."

"Really?" Gwendolyn leaned forward. "Where are they? When will they return?"

"She's not real sure. They were leaving Galveston this morning, but that runaway prince of yours has decided he wants to see a little more of Texas," Hank said with a sneer. "He's draggin' Kerry all over hell and half acre, without a care that she needs to be back here tomorrow for her graduation."

"So you don't think they'll return by Saturday?"

"Mrs. Jacks seemed to think they would. She and Kerry's sisters are drivin' to San Marcus for the ceremony Saturday afternoon." He shook his head. "I sure hope Kerry gets back in time. She's gonna be sorely peeved if she doesn't have time to get ready. She's really lookin' forward to that degree."

"Well," Gwendolyn said in a small voice, watching the condensation on her glass, "she'll still have the degree even if she misses the ceremony."

Hank shot up from his chair. "That prince is makin' me mad. He'd better not do that to Kerry."

"I'm sure she'll tell him how important it is to her."

Hank snorted. "Like he'd listen to some Texas waitress when he's used to bossin' around people right and left."

"Alexi isn't like that. Why do you always think the worst?"

"I do no such thing."

"You already know what I think, Mr. McCauley. This is just more evidence that you're a reverse snob."

"A what?"

"You feel the only worthy people are those who grew up around here...people you know and trust. Well, the world is filled with good, worthwhile people."

"Is that right? Well then why did we get stuck with a prince who won't live up to his responsibilities?"

"He will! He'll be here on Saturday. Why, he could show up at any time."

"We'll see."

HANK SPENT THE REMAINDER of the afternoon on chores around the barn, determined to put Wendy and that damned prince out of his mind. The new bay gelding settled into his stall nicely. His feed had been unloaded and stored, the water buckets were full, and the tack was clean.

His yellow tabby cat, Peaches, deposited a fat mouse on his boot as Hank looked in on his futurity hopeful, a three-year-old chestnut filly who turned on a dime and concentrated like a veteran.

"Good girl." He reached down and praised the cat with long strokes and the silly voice he reserved for her when he was alone. Baby talk, some people might call it. "You're the best mouser in the state of Texas, aren't you?" Reaching down, he grabbed the dead mouse by its long tail, since he knew Peaches expected him to "enjoy" the treat she'd given him.

"Hank?"

The mouse swung like a pendulum from his fingers when he turned around. Wendy screamed like a banshee about the same time Peaches meowed her dis-

pleasure and ran under the bottom board of the stall.
The horse spooked, squealing as the cat dashed across
the sawdust-covered ground for parts unknown.

He stared at Lady Wendy's horrified expressed and
grinned, dangling Peaches's treat from two fingers.
"Welcome to the ranch."

"What are you doing with that mouse?"

"If Peaches had her druthers, I'd sauté it with a nice
cream sauce—kind of like the fish we were served last
night—and present it to her for dinner. But seein' how
it was a gift, I think I'll just find a nice spot to bury
it. It's not a good idea to offend the cat."

A smile replaced Lady Wendy's look of horror. "I
see. No, I can certainly see that honoring her gift is
important for your future relationship."

He shifted away from the stall, watching the shafts
of afternoon sunlight play on Wendy's reddish-brown
hair. "Is anything wrong? I hadn't expected to see you
around the barn."

"Milos Anatole received another call from King
Wilheim. He's threatening to send the royal physician
over if Prince Alexi isn't well by tomorrow."

"Will he do it?"

Wendy clasped her hands in front of her. "Yes."

Hank sighed. "I don't know what to do until Kerry
drives back into town, unless you want to get the
Texas Rangers or the State Highway Patrol involved.
I'm sure I could get a description and a license plate
of her car if you want to notify—"

"No! If we do that, the media will be all over the
place, staking out the hotel in Austin and following all
other leads until Alexi is found. King Wilheim will
know I lied, and then… Well, I just don't want to

admit that I couldn't stop the prince from running off.''

''And ruin your career.''

''King Wilheim would insist I be replaced by someone who had a better control on the situation.''

''That's not fair. I'm sure you didn't just wave goodbye as the prince was drivin' away with Kerry Lynn.''

''No, I tried everything but physically restraining him to no avail.''

Hank grinned. ''If the prince is my size, I don't think you'd have much luck wrestlin' him into the Land Rover.''

Wendy smiled, but she still looked sad and worried. ''No, but I probably should have done something else. Perhaps threatened him.''

''With what?''

''Some old secrets. I could always say I was writing a tell-all memoir of our schooldays together. Or certain holidays with actresses and models.''

''And he'd believe you?''

''Well, perhaps not. But I should have done something.''

Hank wrapped his arm—the one not holding a mouse—around her shoulders as they walked through the barn. ''Quit beating yourself up over this. We can't do a thing until they show up.''

''I feel so helpless…so frustrated.''

He hated how she sounded, all defeated and worried. He knew of only one way to change her mood. ''Well now, darlin', I know just what you need to cure that feelin' ''

She elbowed his ribs. ''Stop it.'' She went through the motions of protest, Hank noted, but there wasn't much passion behind her order or her jab. A slight smile even threatened one corner of her mouth.

"I was thinkin' of something we could do until the sun went down. With all those fox huntin' friends of your daddy, I suppose you've ridden a horse?"

"Yes, I've ridden a time or two."

"Want to go for a ride and a swim?"

"Where?"

"You just have to trust me. This is one of the prettiest sights you'll see around these parts. Heck, in the entire state of Texas! I'd hate for you to miss it."

Wendy smiled. "I'll see if I packed my bathing suit."

Hank gave her his best sober look. "If you didn't, don't you worry. I'll sacrifice my pride and go skinny-dippin' if you will."

His outrageousness made her laugh, and before long he'd buried the dearly departed mouse and saddled two horses.

WENDY DIDN'T KNOW MUCH about where they were going, but evening was rapidly approaching. She might have only one more night in Texas, and she was determined to enjoy it, she decided as she pulled on jeans over her bathing suit. After several days with Hank, she trusted him to show her a good time. He'd taken her out along the Riverwalk in San Antonio, entertained her with stories and his own brand of humor, and tempted her with his kisses. Now she had one last chance to go on an adventure with her Texas cowboy. With a smile, she buttoned her shirt over her black maillot.

She placed a bottle of wine she found in his dining room, along with a corkscrew, a box of crackers and a wedge of cheese from the refrigerator, in a plastic grocery sack she found beneath the sink. From the back of the recliner she grabbed a knitted afghan in stripes of coral, blue and pale green that someone had obviously made several years ago. Almost as an afterthought, she took two towels from the guest bathroom. She wasn't sure where she was going to put all these things on a saddle, but she'd find a way.

"Ready?"

Gwendolyn jumped, then clutched her bundle to her chest. For a big man who wore boots, Hank could certainly move quietly. When her heart slowed, she swallowed and said, "I just put together a few things I thought we might need."

A grin spread over his face as he took in the assortment filling her arms. "Well now, maybe I'd better bring along a pack mule."

Gwendolyn blushed. "It's not that much, really. I thought we might want to…sit down after the ride."

"Right. Well, I'll just bet I can wrap all this into a nice saddle roll."

"Very good, then," she said briskly as he took everything from her, grinning as he noticed the wine and cheese. Gwendolyn shrugged. "It's dinnertime."

"I'd take you out on the town, but everyone at Bretford House, which is the best place in Ranger Springs, would wonder who you are and ask me a dozen questions."

"I understand, truly I do. Staying at the ranch is a wonderful idea. I don't know why I argued with you about it."

"Because you like to argue with me," he replied, his good humor evident in his laughing eyes and contagious grin.

"Perhaps."

"Did you put on sunscreen?" he asked.

"Yes."

In just minutes, Hank had the wine, cheese and everything else rolled inside the afghan and towels. He secured the bundles with pieces of twine from the kitchen. "This can be tied on the back of the saddle." His eyes narrowed as he looked over her body critically. "You have a bathing suit on underneath all those clothes?"

"Yes."

He snapped his fingers and frowned, no doubt teasing her about "skinny-dipping." "Let's go, then. Sunlight's a wastin'."

Gwendolyn followed him to two horses that stood grazing on the tufted grass beside the house. One was a buckskin, the other a flashy pinto. "Won't they run away?"

"They're trained to be drop-tied."

"I see." She didn't, of course, but Hank would probably decline to tell her his training secrets for some silly reason like he'd done before.

"I picked out a nice gentle mare for you, Lady Wendy," he said, walking toward the buckskin. "Why don't you tie that saddle roll on back and I'll give you a leg up."

"This is quite a large saddle," she said as she lay the rolled afghan across the horse's rump.

"It's just your standard western gear."

"I've only ridden English."

"Ah, one of those fancy pieces of leather that's barely big enough to settle your rear into."

"I quite like them."

"You'll like this better. There's even a saddle horn you can grab if you need to."

"Really?"

"Now, this mare neck-reins, which means that you need to hold them in one hand and press them against her neck to make her turn. Press left to turn right. Got it?"

"This is as confusing as your automobiles and highway system."

"Ah, don't worry. You'll get the hang of it."

Gwendolyn walked around the mare, checking the unfamiliar straps and girth. Satisfied the monstrous saddle wasn't going to rotate beneath the horse's belly, she gathered the reins in her hands. "Will you give me that leg up now?"

"My pleasure." Hank came up behind her and placed his hands on her waist. "Now, don't you jump too high."

"Then behave yourself, Mr. McCauley."

Hank laughed as she bent her knee. She expected him to give her a bouncing boost as was common with English riders, but instead he guided one of her hands to the saddle horn—a totally unnecessary encumbrance, in her opinion—and the other to the cantle of the saddle. "Now, just ease on top of Buttercup."

"Really, I'm quite capable—"

"I'm the expert here, remember? You can tell me how to eat asparagus and shake hands with dignitaries, but let me guide you on this one."

Gwendolyn hid her amusement. "Very well."

While she held on to the saddle, he eased her foot into the large wooden stirrup. Then, quite shockingly, he placed his hands on her rear and gave her a boost. She was so startled by the feel of his large, strong hands on her bum that she almost didn't budge. And when she did, she almost overshot the saddle.

Hank chuckled as he adjusted the stirrups. Gwendolyn was about to chastise him when she decided on another tactic. She sat still while he ran his hands over the saddle, the horse and even her own legs. Her skin grew warm beneath the denim of her jeans as he smiled up at her. "She's got a gentle mouth, so you don't need to saw on the reins or pull back hard, okay?"

"I'll try to remember everything you've told me."

"Good girl."

Good girl, my aunt's eyebrows, she thought as he sauntered to the flashy pinto and swung into the saddle. He turned to her and grinned. She managed a tight smile as she adjusted her body to the unfamiliar saddle. Gathering the reins as she saw him do, she nudged the mare with her knees.

First she walked in a circle, getting the feel of neck-reining. Buttercup was responsive, obviously well trained by the smug cowboy who watched her patiently.

"Ready to head on out?" he asked.

"Yes, I believe I am." Putting her heels to the mare and clucking lightly, she shot forward.

"Whoa now, Lady Wendy," she heard Hank shout.

Laughing, Gwendolyn guided the mare into a large figure eight, then stopped her with the slightest pressure of her legs and bit. "She does handle well, Mr. McCauley."

Hank folded his hands over the saddle horn and glared. "You're a ringer, Lady Wendy."

"I'm a what?"

"You tried to fool me into thinkin' you didn't know

much about horses, all the while knowin' you could handle whatever I gave you.''

"I wasn't sure of that. After all, I've never ridden one of these western saddles. I'm accustomed to English, remember, and I jump, not rope cattle.''

"Well, you'll be happy to note that we won't be ropin' any cows today.''

"Fair enough. I'll just ride alongside you, then.'' She tilted her head and gave him a look from the corner of her eye. "If that's all right with you.''

"Fine by me,'' he said, looking slightly suspicious. *Good.* Let him worry about her intentions…and her skills. For once, she'd bested Hank McCauley at his own game!

They rode north out of the ranch area toward some sloping hills covered in blue, yellow and red wildflowers, cactus and other brushy plants. Only a few fluffy white clouds broke the brilliant blue of the Texas sky. The only large trees around were closer to the house, so the horizon seemed infinite. Gwendolyn had never experienced such a feeling of openness as she did under the Texas sky.

"This is really a lovely idea,'' she commented, breaking the near silence of creaking leather and muffled hoofbeats on the dry ground.

"Thanks. I thought you might like to get out.''

"I didn't realize how much until just now. I've been a bit stressed over the situation.''

"Just do me a favor and don't think about all that for now. I'd like to enjoy the evening with a pretty lady and my favorite horse.''

"Well…very good. And thank you.''

He turned and grinned. "You're welcome.''

They rode for a while in silence, keeping the horses

to a walk most of the time, but occasionally breaking into a trot. Gwendolyn resisted the urge to post as she would have in an English saddle. Even if she were going to stay in Texas longer, she doubted she could become accustomed to these large, utilitarian saddles. She much preferred to feel the horse beneath her.

"Is this all your land?" she asked as they topped a rock-strewn hill.

"We're still on my land, but just up ahead is the boundary," he replied, pointing to a stand of trees in a small valley below.

"Is that where we're going?"

"Yep," he said in typical Hank fashion. "It's real pretty. You'll like it."

"I wish I'd brought a camera. The scenery is truly wonderful, rather like the postcards I've seen everywhere."

"Spring is the best time of year in this part of the country. Some people like autumn the best, but I like the wildflowers."

"Do you get much fall color?"

"You mean the leaves turning yellow and red?"

"Yes."

"No. Mostly, the dry leaves just fall off the trees sometime in November. That's what "fall" means around here."

Gwendolyn laughed and guided her mare down the rocky path of sorts. She could tell other horses had been here regularly from the beaten-down, sparse grass, but not lately since she didn't see any fresh hoofprints in the dusty soil.

She followed behind Hank as they entered a wooded area, which she believed was composed of live oaks. They were certainly more stately than the scrubby mesquite trees Hank had pointed out earlier. A wire fence bisected the area, showing the end of Hank's property.

''We need to leave the horses here,'' he said, swinging down from the saddle. He made the movement seem so athletic, so graceful, that she wondered about any injuries he might have received from his former career. He certainly didn't appear to have any weakness, nor did he wince and complain about his joints as she'd been led to believe all cowboys did from the movies she'd seen.

She pulled the mare to a halt, then kicked free of the stirrups. Through the branches she glimpsed a slice of water surrounded by green grass and more rocks.

''When you're riding western, darlin', you usually leave the left foot in the stirrup to dismount,'' Hank said from beside her horse.

''Really?''

He nudged her foot back into the stirrup. ''Just swing your right leg on over and I'll catch you.''

''I don't think that will be necessary.''

He grinned up at her. ''I know, but it sure will be fun.''

She felt herself blush as she followed his orders, trying her best to appear graceful as well as competent. But when she started to hop to the ground, she felt his hands once again at her waist, lowering her slowly. Down his body. Down his hard, lean, muscular body. Slowly.

Down his aroused body.

''Oh, dear,'' she whispered, her legs weak and shaking as she felt his warm breath on her neck.

''Ready for some skinny-dippin'?'' he whispered in her ear. ''Or would you like some of that wine first?''

Chapter Nine

The remainder of Hank's good intentions disappeared once Wendy's round little bottom was pressed against his zipper. How was he supposed to resist *that?* Or the breathy sounds she unconsciously made? Or the soft, feminine way she smelled even when she was out riding horses in ninety-degree heat?

"I believe I'd like a bite to eat," she said softly, interrupting his one-track mind.

"Then that's what we'll do…first," he said, reluctantly pulling away before he made a fool of himself by walking her up against that tree, spinning her around and having his wicked way with her.

She untied one side of the saddle roll while he walked around and released the other. Taking the bundle in one arm, he held out his hand. "The horses will be fine here. Come on."

She placed her hand in his and allowed him to lead them through the grove of live oaks, over the fence that had been bent down from years of abuse—mostly by him—and toward the small pond. The day was perfect for viewing one of his favorite spots in the world, with slanting rays of sunlight filtered through the small live oak leaves, rippling across the still surface of the water. Birds called in the surrounding hills, but here the world consisted of the two of them.

"Oh, it's beautiful," she said with awe. "But who owns this property? Are we going to be in trouble?"

Hank chuckled. "No, we aren't in any trouble. My friend Travis Whittaker owns this piece of land, much to my disappointment. I've been tryin' to buy it from him for years."

"I'm sure he loves it here, too."

"Not as much as I do. At least, I never see him diving into the cold water on a hot summer day."

She looked at him as though she were trying to figure out whether he was joking—and if he wasn't, what he'd look like taking the plunge into the cold water. Playing up what he hoped were some naughty thoughts, he raised his eyebrow and leered. Wendy immediately blushed and looked away, making him smile as he led them closer to the water.

"This little pond is fed by the Edwards Aquifer that's underneath the entire Hill Country. It trickles out into a little stream that eventually empties into the Guadalupe River."

"Is it cold?"

"Compared to a Texas summer, yes. I think it's refreshin', but I'm used to swimmin' here."

"I may try it later."

"Darlin', I sure hope so."

Wendy frowned at him. "Must you do that constantly?"

"What?"

"Flirt outrageously. Make suggestive comments."

"That's just my nature."

Wendy crossed her arms over her chest. "I don't think so. At first I assumed you simply had no regard for women other than as sexual objects, but now that I know you slightly better, I don't believe that's the case.''

"Are you psychoanalyzing me? Because I can tell you right now that's not a good idea. I'm just a simple Texas cowboy. Nothing more, nothing less.''

"Bull," she surprised him by stating. "You are no more simple than I am rich.''

"Well now, I'm not sure about the size of your bank account, but—''

"Don't BS me, Hank. You are far more than a simple Texas cowboy, although for some reason you try awfully hard to make people think you are ill-educated, financially challenged and sexually proficient.''

"Hey, I *am* sexually proficient!''

"Exactly my point!" she exclaimed, throwing up her hands.

"What do you expect me to do, tell you I'm inept in the bedroom? Lady, that's not the case.''

"I didn't mean to imply you were inept, just that you probably haven't had nearly as many partners as you'd like everyone to imagine.''

"You don't know what you're talkin' about," he said, getting angry that she questioned his integrity. Dammit, he'd been mostly honest with her, especially about the things that really mattered.

"So you don't challenge my other observations?''

"I think you're light-headed from not eating dinner, and because I failed to feed you, I take full responsibility.''

"Hank," she said, placing a cool hand on one of his folded arms, "I'm not light-headed. I'd simply like to get to know you better.''

He unfolded his arms. "For how long?"

"What do you mean?"

"You're gonna be out of here as fast as possible as soon as the prince shows up. That might be tomorrow, or the day after at the latest. How well do you expect to know me by then? And why? What reason could you have for psychoanalyzing this Texas cowboy that you're never gonna see again?"

She pulled her hand back and turned away. "You're right, of course. I don't know what I was thinking."

He almost went to her, placed his hands on her shoulders and pulled her against his body. But that would be stupid. He didn't want her peering inside his head or trying to figure out his heart. Some things a man needed to keep private, and his feelings were on the top of the list.

"Let's eat," he said instead, hunkering down and unrolling the afghan. The wine, cheese and crackers tumbled out.

Wendy helped him straighten their makeshift picnic blanket, then spread out the two towels to sit on. As the birds chirped overhead and insects buzzed, they ate in silence. Hank wanted to make some witty comments, but couldn't think of a thing to say. Wendy watched him but didn't try to delve any deeper into his psyche. *Thank goodness.*

Although he began to get a little irritated that she *didn't* try harder to figure him out. Just because he didn't want her to be so nosy didn't mean she should just stop asking her silly questions.

"Did you grow up around here?" she finally asked.

Well, at least she was being nosy again. "Yeah. My father ran a few cattle and had an insurance agency. My mother taught school—junior high."

"Oh? What subject?"

"English."

Lady Wendy smiled, then laughed. "How adorable!"

Hank shrugged. "It's no big deal."

"You made me believe you were this old-fashioned Texas cowboy, as though you lived in nearly primitive conditions, and yet you come from a quite ordinary—or should I say middle-class—background."

"We did okay, I suppose."

"I can see now why education was so important to your mother," Wendy said, placing a small chunk of cheese on a cracker. "She wanted you to have a degree to fall back upon, after your rodeo days, I imagine."

"Yeah, and my father made me invest my money," he grumbled. At the time he'd thought his father was being "ridiculous," as Lady Wendy would say, but now he was glad he'd listened. When he'd wanted to start his ranch, he'd had enough money to make it a first-class operation without being in debt to the bank too much.

"Do your parents still live around here?"

"They moved to the valley—down on the gulf coast—when they retired a few years ago."

"At least they didn't turn their home into a bed-and-breakfast inn," Wendy grumbled.

Hank chuckled, then watched her search the afghan. "What did you lose?"

"I seem to have forgotten the wineglasses."

He shrugged. "I'm willing to share the bottle if you are."

"Oh, that's all right."

"Come on, don't be shy. I don't have any germs you haven't already sampled."

"It's not that—"

"Then there's no problem. Out here in the middle of nowhere, there's not a protocol expert or society matron who's gonna rap our knuckles for not drinkin' from the proper glass."

Wendy smiled. "Oh, very well. I was looking forward to a sip of wine."

He applied the corkscrew after peeling away the covering with his pocketknife. Within a minute he handed the bottle to Lady Wendy. "After you."

"I'd make a toast, but we can hardly clink glasses."

He propped his forearm on his bent knee. "If you were gonna make a toast, what would it be?"

She traced the label with a fingernail, obviously contemplating his question. Then she looked up and raised the bottle. "To a gracious host and a wonderful visit to the heart of Texas."

Hank smiled and nodded. "I'll drink to that."

Wendy took a sip, then handed him the bottle. He watched her eyes as he drank, imagining that he was tasting her, not the crisp Riesling.

"I'd like to propose a toast, too," he said.

She tilted her head and smiled.

"To a true lady who knows more than etiquette and public relations, and who can teach new tricks to even this old dog."

She shook her head and laughed. "I absolutely will not drink to that silly toast. You are certainly no old dog."

"Well, I'm drinkin' to the part about you bein' a true lady," Hank replied with a grin.

"Thank you," she said, accepting the bottle. "At

this rate, I will be a very tipsy lady.'' That didn't stop
her from upending the wine for a long sip.

''A nice swim in the cool water will sober you up.''

She smiled. ''Perhaps.''

''Have a few more drinks of wine and maybe I'll
convince you to take off that bathing suit.''

''I don't think so, Mr. McCauley.''

''Darlin', haven't you ever heard the expression 'he
could charm the birds out of the trees'? Well, at the
moment, I'm more interested in getting you out of
those clothes and into the water.''

THE COOL WATER BECKONED, and in the end, Gwendolyn couldn't resist agreeing to sink into the depths
of the spring-fed pool—wearing her modest bathing
suit, of course. She knew she was more out of her
depth with the man beside her than she would be in
the clear water.

''After you,'' Hank said, reclining on the towel and
afghan like an omnipotent sultan.

''I'll just slip behind the trees, then,'' Gwendolyn
said, gathering her own towel. She was unwilling to
strip in front of him, although he held a much more
liberal view of nudity. Or, in this case, bathing suit
etiquette. Perhaps, she thought with a giggle, she
should have given him a lesson on that subject.

''Something funny, Lady Wendy?''

''Nothing I care to share, Mr. McCauley,'' she said
brightly, hurrying toward the dubious shelter of trees
to slip out of her jeans and shirt. Perhaps she had
swallowed too many sips of wine, although she
doubted that possibility. She was always careful with
alcoholic drinks—except, she remembered with a

frown, when Hank coerced her into drinking more than she'd planned, like that night on the Riverwalk.

Gwendolyn sighed as she reached for the snap on her jeans. She wasn't tipsy, unless her very palpable reaction to Hank could be considered intoxication. Even without his constant teasing and flirting, he made her senses swim. Perhaps a chilly dip in the natural pool would cool her off.

A few minutes later, when she walked to the edge of the water, she revised her opinion. Hank McCauley, stripped practically bare and dripping wet, caused a flood of heat that had nothing to do with the Texas weather.

"The water's cool, but it feels good," he said, sluicing drops from his body with long sweeps of his hands.

I could do that for you. The thought popped into her head quite unexpectedly...and was, she told herself, unwelcome. Except that her body didn't agree.

He wore a pair of faded blue swim trunks that molded to his lean hips and barely covered the tops of his thighs. The elastic sagged so low he appeared in imminent danger of revealing too much of his lower abdomen, where the hair on his chest arrowed down past his navel. Her fingers itched to trace the path, so she curled her hands into fists and stood shivering in the Texas heat.

She tore her gaze away from his wonderful body— all long, lean muscle and golden skin—to the pool. "It looks fabulous."

He chuckled as he walked closer. Her panic increased. She wasn't wearing enough clothing. A thin layer of nylon and spandex couldn't protect her from his hot eyes and roving hands. A state the size of

Texas couldn't protect *him* from her wayward thoughts.

"Jump right in, Lady Wendy. It's not too deep."

Oh, yes it is. I'm in way over my head, she thought as she stood on the edge of a limestone ledge and prepared to jump. To diffuse the situation, she made a snap decision.

Taking a few steps back, she made a short run at the water, rolled her body into a ball and hit the water with a shockingly cold splash. Icy water invaded her bathing suit as she sank below the surface. If she hadn't been concentrating on keeping her mouth shut, she would have gasped at the frigid temperature.

She kicked to the surface, opening her eyes to search for Hank. As soon as she gulped in air, he landed beside her in an even greater splash than the one she'd created.

She treaded water as she waited for him to surface. A wiser move would be to swim away, but she seemed anchored to the spot.

Hank shot out of the water, shaking his head like a wet puppy and laughing breathlessly. "Where did you learn to do a cannonball?"

"Prince Alexi taught me. He learned it while he lived in Boston."

"You surprised me again. Who would have thought a proper English lady could make such a big splash?"

"It was a very proper splash," she said with a cheeky grin.

Hank laughed as he moved ever so much closer, treading water. His fingertips brushed her arm as he moved effortlessly. Heat immediately shot down her body.

"So do you like my swimming hole?"

"Very much," she replied, still sounding out of breath.

"I'm glad." His own voice had turned husky, which caused her to burn even hotter.

"So—"

"Well—"

They laughed together, but then grew quiet, as though neither one could remember what to say. Gwendolyn knew she was incapable of coherent thought. Her whole mind filled with sensations—cold water, and a hot, vivid imagination.

As if he read her mind, Hank bobbed closer, pulling her into his arms. Her pebbled nipples brushed his chest first, shocking her with the sensitive touch. Oh, how wonderful he felt. He was warm and hard, all those glorious muscles and wonderful bone structure suspended in the water for her to explore.

Her hands drifted from his shoulders to his arms, then back again to loop around his neck. He watched her, his hooded blue eyes hot and unblinking. With a sigh, she parted her lips and pressed her mouth against the spot where his jaw and neck met.

Hank gasped and pulled her tight, his legs moving against hers. They seemed at odds, treading first together, then at different rhythms, until they sank lower in the water.

"As much as I'm enjoying this," he whispered hoarsely, "I think it's time to get out of the pool."

"I think you're right," Gwendolyn answered, running her fingers through his thick, wet hair.

She pulled herself away and swam to a low rock, feeling him beside and slightly behind her. She also knew he watched her hoist herself out of the water. Those hours on the StairMaster in the royal workout center paid off, because she knew her thighs and bottom were firm enough to keep from embarrassing herself in the revealing position.

She didn't wait for Hank, but ran on shaking legs to their picnic spot. Grabbing a towel, she hugged it around herself and waited for him to join her.

She had only a short wait. Hank stalked toward her, his feelings clearly revealed for the first time on his expressive face. He wanted her. He was going to have her. Right here, right now, in this shady glade beside the icy pool beneath the wide-open skies of Texas.

The thought thrilled her. At the same time, she felt vulnerable again, shivering despite the heat.

"You're cold," he said as he took her in his arms and pressed her tight. He was hot, aroused. She gasped as he molded his hands over her bottom and pulled her against him until only a few millimeters of wet nylon separated them. Her towel fell to the ground.

"Hank," she whispered.

Her took her parted lips in a kiss that left her head spinning. His tongue eased inside, coaxing a response she was thrilled to give. His kiss was earthy, open and demanding, just like the man himself.

Gasping for air, she broke away and pressed her lips to his shoulder, kissing him, scoring him lightly with her teeth. He groaned and held her tighter, so tight she could barely breathe.

"You don't kiss like a proper English lady," he murmured into her wet hair. His breath teased her neck and she turned toward him.

"And how would you know? Have you kissed many English ladies?"

"Just one, but she's been driving me crazy for the past few days."

"I believe we've been driving each other crazy," Gwendolyn corrected him, snuggling closer. Oh, he felt so good against her skin that she could only imagine how overwhelming the sensations would be if her bathing suit and his trunks didn't separate them. Could she survive the feelings? She entirely hoped so, because she wanted to feel skin against skin, breath to breath, body to body, until nothing separated them.

He took her lips in another heart-pounding kiss that left her light-headed with longing. She rose up on tiptoes to rub against him, running her fingers through his wet hair as he angled his head to deepen the kiss.

"Let me make love to you," he whispered in her ear.

"Yes," she whispered, wanting to be with him more than anything else. Wanting to lose herself in the power of his passion, the charisma of his personality.

He untangled her arms from around his neck and urged her down. Her trembling legs complied as she lowered herself to the afghan. For a moment, Hank loomed over her, giving her a feminine thrill she'd never experienced before. He was so very male that her breath caught.

She'd never dated a man like Hank before—and had certainly never made love to one. He was everything she'd never believed she'd wanted, yet at the same time fantasized about loving. Taming. The rough cowboy. The primitive male. And yet Hank was so different from those stereotypes. He was sensitive to the feelings of others, intelligent and talented beyond her expectations when she'd asked him for help.

He knelt on the afghan, his golden skin dry from the heat that scorched them. For once he wasn't grinning or teasing; he was deadly serious as he reached for the shoulder straps of her bathing suit.

"Yes," she whispered to his unasked question.

His blue eyes blazed as he peeled away the black bathing suit. The stretchy material clung, imprisoning her arms as he pulled it lower, as her breasts were freed to the warm air and his even hotter gaze.

"Magnificent," he said with a slight smile and faint English accent, and she knew he remembered her coaxing to concentrate on a few words Alexi might use. But she wanted Hank's words, not those of her own imaginings, so she levered herself up on her elbows to remove the bathing suit. When she was bare from the waist up, she reached for him.

The feel of his chest, all golden muscles and light brown hair, pressed against her tight nipples. Her softness molded to his hardness, as nature intended, and she reveled in their differences. Who cared that he was Texan and she was English? Who cared that they would never have known each other except for a runaway prince? They were here now, in this shady glade, beneath the cloudless sky as blue as Hank McCauley's eyes.

His leg slipped between hers as his arousal pressed against her thigh, making her groan in longing. He breathed against her neck, his lips caressing the sensitive skin below her ear while her hands roamed the thick muscles of his back. She had never thought of herself as a sensual person, but she wanted to revel in each sensation she experienced in his arms.

Like so many of her experiences in Texas, this was exciting, exhilarating and new. She would store it away, cherish it forever. She knew she'd never meet another man like Hank McCauley, even if she searched forever. The thought brought a tear to her eye, one that she blinked away.

But not rapidly enough.

"What's wrong, sweetheart?"

"Nothing. I just felt...overwhelmed."

"Good overwhelmed or bad overwhelmed?"

She shook her head. "Kiss me. Don't ask me to explain."

He frowned, but she ran her hands over him, pulled him closer and rose to kiss his lips. He surrendered, kissing her in return. His palm closed over her breast and she moaned, begging him to touch her more intimately, to make her forget that she was leaving him very soon. Maybe tomorrow, maybe one more day.

She moaned again, this time more in anguish than passion.

"Wendy?"

"Gwendolyn," she whispered. "My name is Gwendolyn." She wasn't the caricatured English lady he'd teased her about, the one he'd created with a nickname. She had a life, a career, and a family beyond the limited scope of their relationship.

He narrowed his eyes. "What's wrong, sweetheart?"

She closed her eyes and turned away. "I can't do this. I want to be with you. I truly do, but..."

"What?"

"I'm leaving. At first I wasn't thinking about tomorrow, or perhaps the next day, but now I can't get it out of my mind." She opened her eyes and looked at him. "I wanted you to make me forget, but that's wrong."

Hank closed his eyes and rested his forehead against

hers. "I don't want to think about that, either, but can't we have today?"

"I wanted to think we could, but now...I'm not sure."

He lay beside her, still aroused, still incredibly sexy. A part of her wanted to take back her doubts, to hold him close and continue making love. But she'd never been the type of person who could hide from her feelings, or ignore her inner voice.

"Then we'd better go back to the ranch," he said, turning away.

"Hank?"

"Yes?"

"Please don't be angry with me," she said as she pulled the swimsuit over her naked breasts.

"Sweetheart, I'm not angry. Disappointed, maybe, but I'm trying to understand."

Gwendolyn nodded, then smiled sadly. "You've lost your Texas accent again."

Hank tried to smile, but he looked sad, too. "Yeah, maybe I have. But don't you worry, it'll be back."

Just in time for her to leave, she thought as she pushed herself up from the afghan in the hidden, beautiful glade. As the pool shimmered through a veil of tears, and as she began to say goodbye to Hank McCauley.

Chapter Ten

Tension mounted as they neared the ranch. The ride back had been mostly silent, with just an occasional caution or necessary comment to keep them company. He'd looked back several times to make sure Wendy—or perhaps he should start calling her Lady Gwendolyn—was okay, and each time she'd tried to smile convincingly.

He sure as hell wasn't convinced. He wasn't okay. He still throbbed for her. Her taste lingered on his lips while he felt her creamy skin, rather than the worn leather of his gloves, beneath his fingers.

Worst of all, he'd never be able to forget the sight of her lying in his wooded retreat, her whiskey eyes wide and slumberous with desire, her peach-tipped breasts pale and perfect in the filtered sunlight.

"Damn," he muttered as they neared the barn. He'd never be able to see that ugly afghan his aunt Martha had crocheted without thinking of the English lady who had stormed into his life and wheedled her way into his heart.

He pulled his pinto to a halt. "I'll take care of the horses if you'd like to go on in and check the messages."

"Yes, of course," she said, her normally crisp voice without the lively quality he'd come to expect. He didn't offer to help as she swung her right leg over the saddle and eased her left foot out of the stirrup, just as he'd shown her, and jumped to the ground.

"Just push the play button on the machine in my study." He gathered the reins of both horses and started leading them inside the barn.

"I don't want to intrude," she said softly.

He stopped and turned back to where she still stood, looking smaller and more alone than usual against the vivid sunset. "Dammit, Wendy, I won't have any calls on there I don't want you to hear."

His anger apparently gave her strength, because she straightened her spine and glared. "Very well, then. You needn't snap." She turned on her heel and marched toward the house.

Hank narrowed his eyes, knowing this was for the best, but wishing he could charm her out of her huff. Wishing he could put his arms around her and tease her into a smile. But for what purpose? She was leaving tomorrow, or the next day at the latest.

As soon as the prince was found, she wouldn't need him anymore, he reminded himself as he looped the reins of his pinto around a post. Wendy certainly wouldn't want him. He didn't travel in her circles and she didn't belong in his. They were oil and water, and just because circumstances had shaken them up together like a bottle of salad dressing didn't mean anything. The mix was only temporary.

He led her buckskin over to the other side of the barn and tied her there. He seemed destined to have short-term relationships. The buckle bunnies who'd chased him when he was a young up-and-comer had used him for the status he provided. They were the rodeo groupies who attached themselves to the winners with the biggest buckles, the largest money winners on the circuit.

Hank snorted as he unsaddled the pinto. He'd thought, when he was younger, that one particular buckle bunny might really care about him, but he'd been sadly disillusioned when a broken leg had taken him off the circuit for weeks. She'd gone on to the next rising star and he'd learned to guard his heart a little closer.

Since then, there'd been other women who loved to be seen with the champion, and he'd let them hang on to his arm, smile up at him and tell him how great he was. But he didn't believe them. He always tired of them before they tired of him, and everyone had known the score.

He'd been out of his element with Wendy from the start, he reminded himself as he finished grooming the pinto, then started unsaddling the buckskin. Neither he nor the English lady had known what the hell they were doing, just playing every day—sometimes every hour—by ear until that damned prince returned from his unscheduled holiday.

And the whole thing had culminated in a few minutes of sheer madness that should never have happened. He should have put a stop to their attraction before he'd ever touched her creamy white skin or kissed her soft rosy lips. He should have stuck with teasing and not progressed to action. But he didn't have a lot of willpower where Wendy was concerned…and the idea that she was leaving had made him a little crazy.

He led the horses into their stalls, measured out their

feed and filled the water pails. Good honest work and routine, that's what he needed to forget about Lady Gwendolyn. And if he never could go back to the pond and swim without remembering her kisses...then he'd just have to build himself a swimming pool in the back of the house and learn to love chlorinated water over the purity of a natural spring.

Just like he was going to learn to live without the aggravation of a bossy, fussy English lady.

GWENDOLYN CHECKED EVERY phone number and source she could imagine, from Milos Anatole in Austin to the royal secretary in Belegovia to Prince Alexi's mobile phone, but could find no clue to his whereabouts. Except for the call Hank said Mrs. Jacks had received from Kerry, it was as if Alexi had dropped off the face of the earth. She felt defeated, even though she told herself she had one more day before disaster struck.

Perhaps she should tell King Wilheim that Alexi was missing, she thought as she wandered into the kitchen. The uncertainty of the situation caused more stress than almost any reaction she could imagine—except losing her job, of course, and running back to England in disgrace. But she had to think about others, as well. The king would worry incessantly, calling out all types of Texas and United States officials to search for his son. Alexi would be angry because he'd been caught running away from his responsibilities. And Gwendolyn would tender her resignation before she was dismissed because that was the proper thing to do.

She wasn't sure what was proper anymore, especially when it came to two infuriating look-alike men.

Her stomach growled, reminding her she'd eaten

very little that day. Breakfast at the hotel in Austin, no lunch, just a little cheese and crackers beside the pool, followed by several long sips of wine and...Hank.

But she wasn't going to think about him, his kisses or the caresses they'd shared. She'd stay focused on her job, so dedicated that she'd have no time to remember him...or how he'd made her feel.

"Stop it," she scolded herself as she looked into the refrigerator. She needed food, a good night's rest and a wayward prince to get her life back on track.

"There's not much in there," Hank announced, making her jump. Once again she hadn't heard him enter the room because she'd been so caught up in her thoughts.

"I just need a little something. I'm absolutely knackered."

He raised his eyebrows.

"Tired," she translated. "And I'm hungry."

"Why don't I drive on out to Schultze's Roadhouse and pick up some dinner? They have pretty decent barbecue and burgers." He paused, then continued. "I'd ask you to go with me, but I'm still not sure how to explain you to my friends and neighbors."

"I understand." She didn't want to get into Hank's pickup and go anywhere with him, either. She didn't believe she could tolerate the tension that would surely fill the cab, or sit across from him at this "roadhouse" and watch him eat.

Gwendolyn shut the refrigerator, although she would have liked to hide behind the open door forever. "Very well, then. Please get some dinner for me."

"Anything special?"

"Perhaps something with chicken or turkey. I'm sure I'll like whatever you'd recommend."

"I'll do my best."

"Thank you," she said stiffly, almost grimacing at the polite way they now addressed each other. Gone was the teasing, the extravagant accent, the demands that had made Hank so very special.

And tomorrow she'd be gone, so it was for the best.

He grabbed his keys off the kitchen table. "I'll be back in a half hour or so."

Gwendolyn folded her arms across her chest and nodded. Within a minute, she heard the roar of the truck's engine as he backed out, then spun around and rumbled down the drive.

She let out a sigh, then returned to the study. She'd use the time to compose some press releases, just in case Alexi showed up first thing in the morning.

And one just in case he didn't.

BY THE TIME HANK RETURNED with dinner from the pub, Gwendolyn had set the table and made herself a cup of tea. She needed it, she told herself, to calm her nerves and ground her in this foreign land, where everything from the refrigerator in Hank's kitchen to her runaway emotions were bigger than normal.

They managed some small talk about ranch life while she ate smoked turkey in a savory sauce and he devoured a rack of ribs. She learned that he'd bought the ranch five years ago, before he'd thought about retiring, because he'd always loved the land. Around here, he told her, you'd better get what you wanted when it was on the market, because it might not be available again for two generations.

Which made her think about what she wanted...

Certainly not land in Texas, but what about her personal dreams? She'd put everything on hold for her career, which was understandable. She had no steady boyfriend in Belegovia because of her high-profile position; she simply didn't feel comfortable becoming intimate with someone who might talk to the numerous paparazzi hanging around European palaces. She didn't trust anyone to protect her privacy from the press.

Not like she trusted Hank, she thought with a jolt. When had that happened? She tried to remember a time when she didn't trust him, but couldn't think of a single moment. From the first time she'd explained the situation, she'd trusted him not to reveal the secret of Alexi's disappearance. She wouldn't have told Hank otherwise.

And he hadn't disappointed her, not once. He'd behaved admirably in public, except for the suggestive words he'd whispered in her ear at the hospital press conference. And, if he wasn't the model student, then he was at least entertaining. His insistence that life was too short to be serious all the time rang so true when he was tempting her with nights of dancing to country western music, strolling along the Riverwalk, drinking tequila sunrises or talking softly in his hotel suite.

"Finished?" he asked, breaking into her thoughts just when she was on the verge of discovering something important about herself.

"What?" She looked down at her turkey, most of which she'd apparently consumed while she'd been thinking about Hank. "Yes, I am. The meal was delicious. Thank you."

"You're welcome. Would you like dessert? I brought home some peach cobbler. Not made with

Parker County peaches, mind you, which won't be ripe until July, but pretty good, anyway.''

Gwendolyn smiled at the very Hank-like comment. ''Then I suppose I should try some.'' Another Texas experience to savor and store away for the long nights ahead in Belegovia…or in England.

He pushed away from the table, walked across the room and opened the freezer. ''You need some Blue Bell vanilla ice cream or your cobbler just isn't complete.''

''Just a little, please.''

He fixed them both bowls of steaming cobbler topped with scoops of creamy vanilla ice cream. His was twice as large as hers, which was only fitting since his appetite obviously wasn't affected by their strained relationship. Or maybe she was being unfair. Perhaps Hank was better at controlling his feelings, or had more experience handling tension than she.

''This is delicious,'' she said politely as she dipped her spoon into the rapidly melting ice cream. ''If I ever get to Texas again, I'll be sure to try the version with the genuine Texas peaches.''

''You do that,'' he said, staring down into his bowl as if it held the secrets of the universe.

''Well,'' she said, pushing out of her chair and walking to the sink, ''I'd like to take a shower if this is a good time for you.''

He stared at her blankly.

''I don't want to use all the hot water or interfere with your schedule.''

''Don't worry about it.'' His spoon clanked in the dish. ''I'll clean up the kitchen while you take your shower. Take your time.''

Gwendolyn worried what she'd done to make him

turn cool again, but she wasn't going to push the situation into depths she wasn't ready to descend. Hank was entitled to his own feelings. She only wished she understood hers better, because at the moment, she had the strongest urge to go to him, cradle his head against her breasts and apologize for knocking on his door several days ago. Apologize for letting him know how much she'd wanted him just hours ago…and how confused she was because she wanted him still.

THE HOUSE WAS QUIET as it often was this time of night. Outside his open bedroom window, spring insects sang to one another in a natural chorus Hank usually found soothing. Many evenings he'd drift off to sleep, his muscles tired from a full day of honest work, his mind clear of problems, listening to the insects, or sometimes the rain or wind. But tonight he wasn't relaxed and his mind wasn't clear.

He regretted being snippy with Wendy after their meal, but the implication that she might come back to Texas in the future—when they both knew that wasn't true—had irritated him beyond belief. Then she'd thrown out the image of her in the shower and he'd just about lost it. He'd barely been able to talk to her after those comments, retreating to his study while she'd showered and did whatever women did in the bathroom at night.

She'd retreated to the guest bedroom after they'd watched the local news at ten o'clock. She'd seemed tense during the newscast, finally revealing that she worried about ''Prince Alexi coverage''—not that there was anything to cover—and that King Wilheim would expect more newsworthy events from this trip to Texas. In Wendy's mind, this had become a no-win situation, and Hank had silently agreed with her. How could the prince promote his country with the citizens of Texas or the U.S. when he wasn't doing anything to get himself on television? She'd revealed that the prince had had important meetings with business leaders in Dallas before driving to San Antonio—and running off with Kerry Lynn—so at least one part of his trip had been successful.

"Dammit," he muttered, punching his pillow and rolling to his side. He didn't want to think about the prince, especially when he needed to relax, get a good night's sleep and prepare to say goodbye to Lady Gwendolyn Reed.

He listened to the night sounds again, looking across the room to the window. The security lights outside provided full-moon brightness inside. From the guest bedroom he heard the mattress creak, as though Wendy was as restless as he was. She'd probably been thinking about her dilemma, wondering what tomorrow would bring.

Maybe he should give up on sleeping. He could look at the horse auction catalogs for upcoming sales, or balance his checkbook, or—

He heard footsteps. So, Wendy couldn't stay in the bed, either. Maybe they should both get up and play cards, or watch an old movie, or sit around the kitchen table and eat ice cream out of the carton. Anything to keep from thinking about what had happened this afternoon beside the pool. Whenever he closed his eyes, he remembered her face, all flushed with passion, and her breasts, so pretty he'd wanted to spent hours exploring them with his hands and mouth.

Dammit, now he was aroused. Again. He obviously wasn't going to sleep tonight, anyway. With a sigh, he flung back the cover and swung his legs over the side of the bed.

And looked up into the eyes of his English house-guest, the object of his desire, as she stood in the doorway to his bedroom.

He pulled the edge of the sheet over his erection. "Wendy? What's wrong?"

"I couldn't sleep," she whispered hoarsely, as though her voice was rusty from disuse. "I couldn't sleep…because I kept thinking about what happened this afternoon."

Hank ran his hand through his hair, then looked down at his bare feet. "Look, just forget about it, okay? It was a mistake."

"I'm not so sure that's true."

His head snapped up. "What?"

Wendy shifted from one foot to the other. "This afternoon I was frightened that if we'd continued—" she took a deep breath "—if we'd made love, I would regret it when I left."

"And now?"

"Now I think that if we don't make love, I'll regret it for the rest of my life."

Hank let out a breath he hadn't realized he was holding. "Why don't you come on over here and we'll discuss this," he said, patting the bed.

She walked slowly across the room, her feet barely making a sound on the carpet. She didn't resemble the competent, bossy English lady he'd known for merely days. She looked younger, more vulnerable, in her simple white sleep shirt and bare feet. The cool blue light from outside the window washed out much of her color, but even so, she looked pale. Was she worried about what they hadn't done...or what they might do?

She perched on the bed as though she would jump up and run out of his room at any moment.

"You've got to know that I'd love to burn up the sheets with you, darlin'," Hank said, easily falling into his cowboy persona, "but you've got to be sure this is the right thing to do. I don't think my ol' heart could stand it if you put a halt to things after you snuggle into this bed with me."

"I want to go to bed with you."

"And you don't think you'll have regrets in the mornin'?" he asked, tipping her chin up with one finger.

She looked at him directly, so openly he could read the honesty in her dark eyes. "I may have some regrets about things that have happened...decisions I've made, but this won't be one of them." She reached for his hand and squeezed it, as though she was forcing the truth in through his pores. "I promise."

Hank turned, wove his fingers through her hair and kissed her parted lips. She tasted of everything he'd dreamed of for days—elegance and sass, restraint and passion, innocence and seduction. As he deepened the kiss she moaned, her tongue pressing against his, her hands grasping his shoulders, twining around his neck. With a sigh against her lips, he pushed her back onto the mattress.

"No regrets, Gwendolyn," he whispered. "No matter what happens tomorrow."

She nodded, although he thought he caught the glimmer of a tear in her eye. He didn't want tears, so he kissed her eyelids, then her cheeks. Her skin was smooth and tasted the way vanilla smelled. They rolled together until she was twisted in the sheet and he was lying half on top, completely uncovered.

Her hands roamed his body, arousing him with long strokes of his back and short grasps of her nails. When she got to his waist, she pulled her head back and looked at him.

"What are you wearing?"

"Not a blessed thing," he whispered. "And you're wearing way too much." He grabbed the hem of her sleep shirt and pulled it up past her thighs, although he didn't want to stop kissing her long enough to get her completely undressed.

She rolled them over, tangling him once again in the sheets, but at the moment, he didn't care. She sat up, reached for the shirt and whipped it off in a graceful arc.

She wasn't wearing a blessed thing, either. Hank smiled. "Nice."

"Thank you," she said primly before leaning over him, brushing the tips of her breasts against his chest and searing him with a kiss that went on forever.

He grasped her bottom and pulled her on top so she straddled him. He took advantage of the situation to run his hands over her breasts, her waist, her hips, memorizing the feel of her. When she moaned and collapsed on top of him, he rolled them over until they were perilously close to the edge of the bed.

Lacing their hands together, he looked into her eyes. "Stay with me," he whispered, not knowing what he meant, only knowing he had to say the words.

"All night," she replied breathlessly, and he knew that was all either of them could promise.

He worked them back toward the head of the bed, closer to the nightstand drawer where he kept protection. He couldn't get enough of her kisses, her caresses. And he couldn't stop himself from touching her everywhere, from her sleek, lustrous hair to her firm, smooth legs. And in between, where she was damp for him. Where she gasped and silently asked for more.

He complied, sending them both soaring, holding nothing back as their bodies joined. She arched against him, seeking a rhythm, and he tried to go slow. He wanted this first time to last forever, but her throaty moans and demanding hands were driving him crazy. When she convulsed around him and sank her teeth into his shoulder, he let himself go, surrendering with a shudder of completion that left him breathless and dazed.

Reality came back slowly. The rasp of Wendy's hot breath against his neck, the smell of mind-blowing sex surrounding them, the gentle May breeze caressing his bare backside. Outside he heard the crickets and other night insects singing to one another.

"I must be crushing you," he whispered.

"No. Stay," she said faintly, but accented her command by closing her arms around him and holding tight.

"Spoken like a true aristocrat," he said with a chuckle, moving his hips against her, making her gasp. "I'll do my best to please my lady."

"Oh, you do," she said breathlessly before he turned and kissed her again.

Chapter Eleven

"What the heck is going on?" Dr. Ambrose Wheatley asked as he stood inside the Four Square Café and gazed out at the town square. Two odd-looking strangers argued with each other. Both of them had at least two cameras hanging around their necks.

"Beats me," Travis Whittaker said, only half interested since his bacon and eggs had just arrived. "Maybe they're lost."

"I don't think so," Thelma, the newspaper owner and editor, stated as she walked to the window. "Maybe I should go see if they need some help."

"Might be a good story in it," Dr. Wheatley replied with a chuckle. Since he'd semiretired last year after his daughter returned to take over his practice, he had a lot more time to socialize with his friends and pester his new wife, Joyce, at her hair salon.

Travis buttered his biscuits and tried not to get involved in the scene unfolding outside.

"Maybe they're government agents," Jimmy Mack Branson added as he joined two of the busiest busybodies in town.

"I don't think so, not with those cameras. Undercover types don't usually take pictures, do they?'' Ambrose asked. ''But they do look a mite suspicious.''

Travis sighed. He should have sat in one of the booths at the back, but instead had chosen his favorite table by the plate-glass window overlooking the park-like town square with its gazebo and flowering bushes.

He glanced outside again. The older man wore a wrinkled, cheap suit and had a five o'clock shadow left over from last night. The younger man wore baggy khaki pants and a multipocket camouflage vest. One of his cameras boasted a lens that could photograph a horsefly from the next county.

''Maybe they're professional photographers. They could be taking pictures of the bluebonnets,'' Jimmy Mack said.

''Then what are they doing in our town square?'' Thelma asked. ''I'd better go ask them if they're lost.''

''Good idea,'' Travis said. ''Ambrose, you might want to go with her for backup, just in case they decide to take her in for interrogation.''

Jimmy Mack frowned. ''I'd better go open the hardware store. It's nearly ten.''

The doorbell tinkled merrily as everyone left. Travis smiled and took a big bite of eggs.

He'd just buttered his last biscuit and topped it with strawberry preserves when Thelma burst into the café, her tight gray curls bobbing and her eyes alight with *news* in thirty-point type.

''One of them is a tabloid photojournalist,'' she announced to anyone who was paying attention, ''and the other one is a paparazzo from one of those sleazy European rags.''

''What are they doing in Ranger Springs?'' Travis

had to ask, despite his best intentions to mind his own business and finish his breakfast.

"For some reason, they're looking for Prince Alexi of Belegovia in *our town*. Can you imagine? Like the prince is going to come here on his important state visit when everyone knows he's in Austin, waiting to hear if the president is coming to Crawford for the weekend."

"They could be some of the same paparazzi that chase movie stars and royalty, trying to photograph their weddings," Mrs. Jacks stated, carrying a plate of hotcakes and sausage to Pastor Carl Schleipinger. "There should be laws against those people harassing everyone who is the least…bit…famous." She plopped the plate in front of the minister and sat down in an empty chair.

"Mrs. Jacks, are you all right?" Pastor Carl asked.

Thelma hurried over. "You look as though you've seen a ghost, Charlene."

"It's the royal thing," Dr. Wheatley said, hurrying over to take her pulse. "Charlene, do you feel dizzy?"

"What?"

"How do you feel, dear?" Thelma asked, patting her other hand. "Dr. Wheatley wants to know."

"Oh, I'm fine now. I just…thought of something."

"Yes, we know," Dr. Wheatley said. "It's that royalty thing."

She looked at him blankly. Travis suspected something other than the princess's untimely death several years ago was bothering the middle-aged waitress, but darned if he knew what. He'd heard from friends that she was a royal buff; she'd even wanted to go to Queen Elizabeth's Silver Jubilee in London this year, but Kerry was graduating and they really didn't have the money for that type of trip.

"I swear, Charlene, you gave me a fright," Thelma said.

"I'm better now, but I think I'll rest for another few minutes in the office."

"I could drive you over to the clinic," Dr. Wheatley offered. "Amy is still seeing patients until one o'clock."

"No, I'm fine. Really. I'll just splash some water on my face and put my feet up for a few minutes."

She stood with the help of Pastor Carl and the doctor, smiling weakly at both men. "You help yourself to more coffee until I get back."

"Don't worry about us," the minister said.

Travis decided he needed another cup, so he retrieved the carafe and refilled his and the pastor's. Glancing outside, he noticed that the two reporters had stopped arguing and were walking toward the café.

"Here comes your story, Thelma," he said.

The bell tinkled gaily as the two men entered. One had the darker coloring of southern Europe or perhaps northern Africa, while the other looked like a hard-drinking, heavy-smoking journalist from a 1940s black-and-white movie. Both of them tried to look pleasant as they stopped just inside the door.

"Hello," the older one said in a gravelly voice and Bronx accent. "We were just wondering if anyone here knew where we could find a man named Hank McCauley."

"THERE ARE TABLOID reporters in Ranger Springs," Hank told Gwendolyn when he hung the phone. "And they're looking for me *and* Prince Alexi."

"Oh, no!" She sank back on the couch, all the starch gone from her spine. Her worst fear—other than losing her job—was negative publicity. This type of scandal was just what the paparazzi were looking for. They'd love to break the story of the missing prince, his working-class lover and the phony prince that had dined with congressmen and the governor of Texas. Add a two-headed baby and an alien abduction and they'd have a bestseller. She dropped her head to her hands and felt like crying.

"Who was that on the phone?" Gwendolyn asked, her voice muffled as she rubbed her aching head.

"Mrs. Jacks. She was calling me from the office of the café, telling me they were looking for the prince. Then Thelma rushed in and told her they were looking for me, too."

"Then they'll be looking for me, too. Oh, this is terrible."

"They don't know anything yet."

She looked up into Hank's frowning face. "But they will. These…maggots are so persistent. And they'd sell their own mothers for a story. You have no idea how utterly ruthless, how reprehensible, they are."

"Not your favorites," he said dryly. "Okay, then let's assume they'll eventually find out how to get to my ranch. We'd better not be here when they arrive."

"But where would we go that we'll be safe from them and still be able to get in touch with Kerry and Prince Alexi when they *finally* show up?"

"Mrs. Jacks is gonna do her best to contact Kerry Lynn and the prince and warn them to stay away from town. And she's telling the paparazzi a story about seeing someone who looked like the prince in a car at the Dairy Queen in Buda, which is out on Interstate 35.''

''Does Mrs. Jacks think the paparazzi will believe this story?''

Hank shrugged. ''Who knows? But it's the best we can do for now. There's another possibility, one we haven't considered until now.''

''What's that?''

''That Kerry Lynn is running late, probably because the prince decided to take another detour,'' he added with contempt, ''and she needs to drive directly to the graduation ceremony.''

''So we're going to her university?''

Hank nodded, then glanced at his watch. ''I think it's the only other place she might show up besides her house or where her momma works in Ranger Springs. We should have plenty of time to discover where the graduates are dressing, where the guests are sitting and so forth.''

''Is the school far away from here?''

''About a half hour to forty minutes,'' Hank told her, pulling her up from the couch, ''so you'd better get a move on. Wear something kind of casual—not one of those cold-weather power suits you're so fond of—but not your jeans, either. And wear comfortable shoes because we may have to do a lot of walking.''

And *he* talked about *her* being bossy? ''Very well. Anything else?''

''Put some sunscreen on your nose,'' he said with a smile, giving it a tweak.

Just like that, she went from being slightly peeved to hopelessly smitten. How did this infuriating man make her emotions leap to extremes with the crook of his finger? In the past twenty-four hours she'd experienced tenderness, exasperation, frustration, desire and a dozen other feelings too jumbled to name.

Just thinking about the *desire* part...she wanted to crawl back into his large bed, pull the covers over them both and hide from the world for the next forty years or so. Maybe by then she'd become tired of his fantastic body, or annoyed with his teasing, or bored with his intelligence. Maybe then she could go about her life without constantly thinking of Hank McCauley.

"I've got to call Milos Anatole and tell him what's happening," Gwendolyn stated, trying to get her thoughts together on her job, not her personal life.

"It might be a good idea to have Pete Boedecker drive him in from Austin, just in case the prince shows up."

"You're right. I'll have Pete prepare the Land Rover and pick him up." She frowned. "But where could they stay where they won't alert the paparazzi?"

"Tell them to get a room in San Marcus, although it won't be easy with all the friends and family in town for the graduation. If they look around, they ought to be able to find a motel that isn't too crowded where they can park the Land Rover in back."

Gwendolyn was absolutely certain Milos would not be happy about checking out of the grand historic hotel in Austin to find a room that no one else wanted in a small college town, but she couldn't help the situation. Hank's suggestion made a lot of sense.

Forty-five minutes later, they parked the small pickup truck Hank had borrowed from Juan—just in case the reporters knew what his dually looked like— in the guest parking lot for the graduation ceremony. They were early, but as Hank had mentioned, they needed to explore the possible ways Kerry Lynn Jacks and Prince Alexi could enter the facility.

"I'm really not sure the prince would take part in such a public venue, even if he felt he was disguised."

Hank gripped her hand and they started walking. "Who knows what this guy might do? All we know is that he won't answer his damn phone or give you a call."

That was true, but Gwendolyn didn't want to start listing Alexi's faults again, especially when Hank had added several new traits to the list. She decided to concentrate on walking beside Hank, hand in hand, as though they were a carefree couple out to see a family member or friend graduate. What could be so difficult about that?

They'd certainly done more than hold hands last night. She'd acted like a woman possessed, unable to keep her hands off Hank, unable to stop kissing him until they were both breathless. She'd never thought of herself as sensual, but in his arms, she felt as sexy as Madonna and as powerful as Oprah Winfrey. He'd been the most generous, the most glorious lover she could ever imagine. Her previous experiences paled in comparison to this marvelous joining of heart and body.

Even if it was temporary. Even if she did plan to leave Texas as soon as possible.

"If we see anyone I know, just smile and try not to say anything. If they ask you a direct question, you can tell them your name is Wendy and that you're a…flight attendant or something."

"A flight attendant?" She laughed. "Do you actually think I look like a flight attendant?"

"Sure. One of those classy ones on British Airways.

Not Virgin Atlantic, mind you. That just sounds too weird.'' Hank nodded. ''Yeah, a British Airways flight attendant. We met at a party in Austin—mutual friends and all that.''

''What in the world would a flight attendant from British Airways be doing in Austin? We hardly fly there, you know.''

''Well, then, Dallas. I go up there every now and then.''

''Very good. And have we been dating long?''

''Naw. You don't get to town often, but when you do, you're hot to see me.''

''Oh, I am?''

He flashed her a grin. ''Absolutely.''

Gwendolyn laughed. Pretending with Hank was fun, something she hadn't expected today. With last night's passion and this morning's tabloid reporters breathing down their necks, the atmosphere should have been serious and tense. But then, when had she ever been able to anticipate what Hank would do or say?

''Just remember to cling to my arm and look up at me with adoration in those whiskey eyes of yours.''

''Whiskey eyes? I'm not sure that's very flattering.''

''Darlin', believe me, that's real flattering. You've got genuine 100-proof, hickory-aged, finest Kentucky bourbon eyes if I've ever seen them.''

Gwendolyn laughed, then clung to his arm and looked up into his teasing blue eyes, batting her eyelashes and hoping she looked besotted. ''How's this?''

Hank narrowed his eyes and evaluated her critically. ''No, that's not quite right. I'm afraid anyone could see right through you.''

''Oh.'' She'd actually thought she was being a

clever actress, but she hardly stood a chance against Hank McCauley.

"We need to make this a little more genuine." He placed his hands on either side of her head, sliding his fingers into the hair at her temples. "Hold on, darlin'."

He kissed her then, while her lips were still parted and her mind frozen by his charm and good looks. She closed her eyes and groaned, easing her arms around his waist and grasping his hard, sculpted back with her hands. Hank was an expert kisser, but he added something beyond skill. Passion, sincerity and caring were part of the caress of his lips and tongue, and she never wanted it to end. Her head began to whirl. Slowly, she became aware that he was holding her tightly or she would have dissolved into a puddle on the concrete sidewalk.

As his lips eased from hers, she clung a moment longer, not wanting the contact to end. She felt so alone when he wasn't touching her, she realized. She'd lived within her skin for twenty-nine years, and yet now she needed Hank to feel complete. Although the feeling didn't make sense, she accepted it for what it was: a woman's basic instinct to bond with a man— in this case, a very attractive, very virile man who made her feel things she'd never imagined.

She had the strangest desire to grip the fabric of Hank's shirt and pull those pearl snaps apart, which was probably the reason cowboys wore them. Easy access to hard-muscled flesh and smooth, warm skin.

"Now you look like someone who's hot to see me," he said, his own voice a little shaky. He combed his fingers through her hair and smiled down at her. "I'm sure glad you're here."

"As the British Airways flight attendant or as the public relations director in hiding?"

"Just as you, Lady Wendy. Just you," he said, lowering his head and kissing her gently again.

He took a deep breath, then said, "I guess we'd better start searching for Kerry Lynn and your runaway prince."

Gwendolyn nodded, but inside she disagreed. Alexi wasn't her prince; Hank was. He'd become the fantasy she'd never dare dream, the ideal man who made her feel like a woman. And he was so temporary, just a short detour in the course of her life. She didn't want to think of leaving him so soon, but she must. She had duties and long-held goals that couldn't be denied.

For today, she'd pretend to be that British Airways flight attendant who was so besotted with her Texas cowboy. She didn't need to be much of an actress to pull it off.

THEY MANAGED TO GET GOOD seats near an aisle, so they could both look for Prince Alexi and beat the crowd to the graduates to talk to Kerry Lynn. Hank looked around for Mrs. Jacks and Kerry's two sisters, but didn't find them in the crowd. No telling where they were sitting; this wasn't exactly like a football game, where the "visitors" sat on one side and the home team on the other. But it didn't really matter where her family was as long as she was on that stage and the prince was watching from someplace close by.

Sitting patiently wasn't Hank's strong suit. He wished this was a sporting event so he could get a soft drink and some nachos. Instead, he fidgeted in his seat, stretching his legs out past the metal railing and shifting his weight from hip to hip until Wendy gave him a hard glare.

"I'm nervous enough without you making me crazy," she whispered.

"Sorry. I'm just ready for this ceremony to begin." He glanced at his watch. Any moment now he'd see Kerry march in. He scanned the audience. Where was the prince? Or had she dropped him off someplace? Maybe he didn't care enough to watch Kerry Lynn graduate...the cad.

Just when Hank had worked up a head of steam over the prince, the graduates filed out of the back-stage area to the folding seats set up down below. Wendy leaned forward, her eyes intent on the audience while Hank watched the graduates. He wasn't sure what order they'd sit in, so he had to look at every young, fresh face. Kerry Lynn might be a few years older, but she didn't look it. And with her petite figure, she'd be hard to spot.

She came in between a lineman-size guy and a tall redhead. Hank watched her take her seat and breathed a sigh of relief.

"She's here. Do you think the prince is around?"

"I imagine he is. For one thing, I doubt he has anywhere else to go, since she is driving. And also, attending her graduation would be the polite thing to do."

Hank snorted, focusing on Kerry Lynn. She sure looked okay. Happy, even. Kind of radiant. He supposed achieving her goals had made her feel pretty good about herself.

Suddenly she waved, her attention focused across the auditorium. Hank nudged Wendy, but when they both looked at the attendees seated there, there was no prince. Instead, Mrs. Jacks and her two other daughters waved cheerfully at Kerry Lynn.

Hank settled back while Wendy continued to scan the crowd. There wasn't anything to do until the ceremony was over. Then he'd find Kerry and make her tell him where the prince was hiding.

But when the graduates had received their diplomas, turned their tassels to the other side of their cap and marched off to find their families, Hank suspected they'd been outfoxed by a petite blonde and a crafty prince.

Hank pulled Wendy through the crowd to find Mrs. Jacks, Kerry's younger sisters, Carole and Cheryl, and Carole's daughter, Jennifer. After he introduced Wendy, the British Airways flight attendant, to the other ladies, he asked, "Did you have anything planned with Kerry Lynn today?"

"No, we'll have our regular family dinner tomorrow after church, and then a little party for Kerry and her friends in the afternoon. I thought you'd gotten your invitation, Hank," Mrs. Jacks said.

"It must have slipped my mind," he answered, thinking about the stack of unread personal mail on his desk. "So, you don't have any idea where she might have run off to?"

"I just can't imagine," Carole said, frowning. "Why isn't she here with us now?"

Mrs. Jacks fidgeted with her purse strap. "Maybe she has some friends waiting for her. Or a good friend," she added.

"Where?" Wendy asked, leaning forward. Hank knew she was anxious, but now that Kerry Lynn had attended her graduation ceremony, he wasn't in any hurry to find the prince.

"I have no idea," Mrs. Jacks replied.

"I sure would like to congratulate her on her graduation. If you hear from Kerry, please ask her to call me," Hank said, tugging on Wendy's hand before she asked any more questions in front of Kerry's two inquisitive sisters and young niece.

"Nice to meet all of you," Wendy said as he pulled her away from the Jacks family.

"That was rather abrupt," she said breathlessly after they stepped out of the flow of folks hugging and smiling with the graduates.

"Sorry, but I was afraid you might sound suspicious to her sisters if you asked anything else."

Wendy took a deep breath and sighed. "I suppose you're right. I was just so sure we'd find them…"

WENDY INSISTED THEY WAIT until everyone had left the auditorium, just in case Kerry Lynn and the prince materialized, so they stood around and said hello to a few folks he knew. Wendy played her role of adoring flight attendant to perfection. Although he knew he'd conditioned her to react in a believable manner, he felt as if he was looking into the eyes of someone who really cared for him as a man and not as a former champion or a "good catch" among the other cowboys of the area.

But he'd felt like this before, from the first buckle bunny who'd grabbed on to his belt loops at age seventeen, to the last one who'd amicably departed after he'd bought her a new custom saddle with silver conchos. He'd always *wanted* to believe women were sincere where he was concerned, but he'd learned that either they were deluding themselves, or downright lying to get whatever they could from him.

Lady Wendy had always made it clear that she needed him for one purpose—pretend to be the prince. But what had happened beside the pool and continued last night in his bedroom had nothing to do with his "duties" to impersonate the prince. There had been a depth of emotions involved in their relationship that went far beyond easing an itch that needed to be scratched.

Wendy hadn't needed or wanted just any man; she'd wanted *him*. And Hank knew he couldn't forget that fact, no matter if or when the prince returned, no matter whether Wendy returned to Belegovia today, tomorrow or next week. He knew he'd feel the same way about her next month, next year, and that scared all the "aw, shucks" and "gee, ma'am" one-liners right out of him.

When no one had exited in ten minutes or so, he said, "Let's go get some dinner. We haven't eaten anything since breakfast, and although that prince has almost killed my appetite, we need to keep up our strength."

Wendy nodded. They walked hand and hand back to Juan's pickup. "I think I'll call Juan and see if anyone approached him in my dually, or if anyone has been around the ranch."

"Good idea. I'll call Milos and see if he and Mr. Boedecker managed to find a room here in town."

They spent a few minutes on their respective cell phones at the truck. Wendy finished first, then leaned against the Nissan's fender and waited for him to hang up.

"Okay, thanks, Thelma. I appreciate the information."

"What did you discover?"

"The reporters know about Kerry Lynn. I'm not sure how, but they're convinced the prince is in Ranger Springs, having a torrid affair with a local waitress."

"That sounds just like the paparazzi, only their headline would be more insulting."

"I think maybe Thelma cleaned it up, considering it's a local girl they're talkin' about." Hank shook his head. "Damn that prince."

Wendy put her hands on her hips. "And what about Kerry Lynn Jacks's responsibility? The prince didn't force her to take him with her. All he did was ask and she jumped at the opportunity."

"That's bull! You make her sound like she's some gold digger. She's not."

"I never said any such thing!"

"You need to be angry at the person who caused this mess. *Your* prince."

"He's not *my* prince. He's my friend."

"Right. And at the moment, you're as mad as a hornet over his behavior."

"Oh! Right now, it's you I'm angry with. You and your Kerry Lynn."

"She's not my Kerry Lynn!"

"So you say," Wendy said in a huff. She crossed her arms over her chest and glared at him. "I think you're still smitten with her."

"Smitten?" Hank shook his head and scoffed. "That's the craziest thing you've said. I already told you about Kerry Lynn and me."

"You seem awfully concerned for someone who's just a friend. Or was it more like a big brother?"

Hank put his hands on his hips and glared. "A big brother, and yeah, I care. She doesn't have a brother, or a daddy, or any other man to stand up for her. She's helped support that family for years and she deserved to walk across that stage and get her diploma. She deserves happiness more than any of those pampered kids who had Mommy and Daddy pay for everything.''

Wendy still didn't look convinced, although she was weakening. ''Besides, taking care of one another is what we do around here. Looking out for our friends, being family even though we aren't related by blood. That's what living in this small town is all about, and I'll be darned if I let you put some kind of twisted meaning to it because you're jealous.''

Wendy looked at him with her eyes wide, then her bottom lip started to tremble. To his shock, tears sprang to her eyes and her face fell.

''Dammit, don't cry,'' he said softly as he pulled her in his arms.

''I can't help it,'' she sobbed. ''You're right. You're so right.''

''I was angry.''

''But you're right. I'm so jealous I can't think straight.'' She sniffed against his shirtfront. ''Not of Kerry Lynn and you, although that's what I thought at first. I'm really jealous of the way everyone cares for everyone else. How your friend took care of your ranch, how you talk about Mrs. Jacks. The picture you painted with your words about how everyone looks out for one another.'' She gulped in a breath of air and sobbed, ''I want to feel that way.''

''Ah, Gwendolyn. Ah, honey,'' he whispered as he held her tight. He didn't know what to say in the face of such naked emotion. He'd thought of her as competent, talented and sexy, but he hadn't seen the little girl inside who was still looking for her father's approval and her family's support. To her, Ranger Springs must seem like heaven on earth.

"I'm sorry," she whispered.

"Don't you apologize. You're entitled to your feelings."

Her hands held tight to his back. "You're a very nice man, you know that?"

He felt a little misty-eyed at the moment. "Don't you tell that to anyone else, you hear?" he teased to ease the feelings. "Now, why don't we get some food and forget about Kerry Lynn and Alexi for a few hours?"

"That sounds wonderful."

"I'll have Juan drive over to the ranch and we can exchange pickups later tonight."

"Okay."

He rubbed her shoulders while she rested her cheek against his shirt. "You know the best thing?"

"No. What?"

"We get to spend another night together."

She looked up at him, blinking away the tears she'd shed moments ago. "There is that," she whispered.

Chapter Twelve

The cell phone rang just as they were leaving San Marcus. Gwendolyn checked the caller ID on the display, but all it read was Out of Area. With a trembling finger, she pressed the answer button.

"Lady Gwendolyn, is that you?"

"Yes, Your Majesty," she said in her professional voice. The one she hadn't used for hours, maybe days.

"I have received some alarming news from the information officer at the palace. Let me read you the headline—Prince Seduces Schoolgirl Waitress. According to an Internet Web site, my son is having a torrid affair with a young woman in some small Texas town I've never heard of before. Ranger Springs, I believe. The article says she is a waitress at a truck stop and attends school at a nearby college. This headline makes my son sound like a child molester!"

Gwendolyn winced. "I assure you, King Wilheim, your son is not in Ranger Springs conducting an affair with anyone."

"The Web site has photos!"

"Really? Well, it just so happens that I know the true explanation," she replied, crossing her fingers. "That is actually a photo of a local horse trainer and former rodeo cowboy named Hank McCauley. He bears a remarkable resemblance to Prince Alexi, and his former girlfriend is a twenty-eight-year-old woman who is graduating from the university just this weekend.''

She imagined him perusing the photo as silence continued on the phone line. ''Have you seen this Hank McCauley?''

She hesitated a moment, thinking of all the ways she'd seen Hank. Laughing, studious, irritated, teasing…naked. ''Yes, I have.''

''And you can assure me that it is he, not my son, who is in this photograph?''

''Absolutely, Your Majesty.''

She imagined him nodding, a frown on his high forehead. ''Very well, then. We will issue a press release from here at the palace. Alexi needs to make an appearance immediately, even if he must be lifted from his sickbed. Do you understand?''

''Yes, Your Majesty.''

''An appearance with this Hank McCauley would be even better. Call the man and see if you can arrange it.''

''I'll do my best.''

''Yes, I know you will. We must not let this scandalous inference get out of hand. The paparazzi will hound us to death if they sense a weakness. Right before Alexi makes his choice of a bride is not the time to link him with a scandal.''

''I totally agree, Your Majesty. I will talk to Mr. McCauley and contact you immediately when I have arranged something.'' She just hoped the ''something'' she arranged was not a statement that the prince was indeed missing...with the "schoolgirl" waitress.

"Good. We are depending on you, Lady Gwendolyn."

"I know, Your Majesty, and I appreciate your trust."

She ended the call when the monarch said goodbye, then leaned her head back against the seat.

"Bad news, hmm?"

"A photo that I assume is of you and Kerry Lynn is now posted on an Internet Web site specializing in royal scandals. It was brought to King Wilheim's attention, and since it is past midnight right now in Belegovia, I assure you he is extremely upset about the scandalous accusation that Prince Alexi has seduced a schoolgirl who also works as a waitress."

"Damn."

Gwendolyn closed her eyes. "My sentiments exactly."

THEY STOPPED FOR MEXICAN food at an out-of-the-way family-owned restaurant in a little town that probably wasn't on the map. Hank had said he was going the "back way" to Ranger Springs and Gwendolyn felt thoroughly lost. Not that she needed to know where they were going, she told herself. Since Alexi hadn't shown up, she had nowhere to go, nothing to do except wait for the other shoe to drop. She certainly didn't need to spend hours "finding" Hank and "convincing" him to cooperate in a joint press conference.

The late afternoon was hot, but then, the weather had been hot and dry for the entire trip, so that wasn't anything new. Somehow she wished the sun had already set so they would be more invisible to the paparazzi and tabloid reporters. If two of them were in Ranger Springs this morning, more had probably shown up by now. She hadn't shared that piece of information with Hank, however, because it wouldn't do any good to worry or upset him. He'd been such a champ about this situation, going well beyond his duty to help her search for the prince and avoid negative publicity.

Hank knew the family who operated the restaurant, so she suspected he came here regularly. He also ordered for her, an action which usually irritated her when men made that assumption, but tonight barely caused a ripple.

"What did you order?" she asked when the short, cheerful woman with dark hair and eyes left for the kitchen. Hank had called out names for the platters based on Texas cities along the border with Mexico.

"A sour cream chicken enchilada, a cheese enchilada with red sauce, and a crispy beef taco, with refried beans and rice."

"That sounds like a lot of food."

"We haven't eaten since breakfast and I wasn't sure what you liked. Have you ever eaten Mexican food before coming to Texas?"

"No, except for the nachos along the Riverwalk. There are a few restaurants in London now. I'm sure it's different here in Texas."

"Probably. I'm havin' a hard time picturin' Tex-Mex served with a British accent, but I suppose it works," he drawled, obviously trying to lighten the mood.

Gwendolyn looked at him across the table, where a bottle of beer sat by his plate and a glass of sangria waited for her to sip. The restaurant situation wasn't so different from the two of them, she thought. Texas and Great Britain locking horns, so to speak, at every opportunity. Misunderstanding each other on occasion. But could they coexist, even thrive, like the Mexican restaurants in London?

And why was she even thinking these thoughts when she would be leaving, one way or another, very soon?

"Thank you again for your patience," she said. "Today was futile, but you're right. We had no place else to search."

"What are you going to do if he doesn't show up tomorrow?"

Gwendolyn sighed and picked up her wine. "I suppose I'll have to admit the truth to King Wilheim, then contact the authorities."

"We could run something by Ethan Parker first if you'd like. He's the chief of police and a personal friend. He might have some ideas."

"Thank you, but I'd rather not involve anyone else, especially someone who might be obligated to report the prince as missing."

Hank frowned. "I don't think Ethan—"

"Please, let's just drop the subject for now. I don't want to think about the prince or his continued disappearance." She took a sip of the sweet wine, then rested her forearms on the table. "You were right about me being angry with him, but I'd also like to understand why he does these foolish things. It's almost as if he's trying to get into trouble."

"Maybe he wants to get caught."

"I don't know. Perhaps getting engaged and eventually married will settle him down."

Hank snorted in a most unbelieving manner. "That

just doesn't happen. Women want to believe it does, but marriage never settled anyone down who didn't want to commit to one woman and one bedpost where he can rest his hat.''

She tilted her head and studied him. "Is that why you've never married? You've never felt the urge to settle down with one woman?"

"Darlin', I'm pretty settled. I have my own ranch, I built my own house, and it's sort of decorated. I have a good life, and just because I don't have a wife to interfere with my horse training and traveling doesn't mean I'm shiftless.''

"I didn't mean to imply you were shiftless. I just wondered why you've never found one woman to share your life."

He was obviously uncomfortable with the subject, leaning back in his chair and taking a long swallow of beer. Finally he plunked the bottle on the table. "Okay, I admit I've never found the right woman. But I'm not lookin', either. When I start lookin', I'll find someone, but I have some pretty strong standards."

"I believe you."

"Women complicate things," he explained, frowning at the bowl of chips and salsa on the table. "They want to change you, and they want you to prove you love them."

"Really? I've never really thought about relationships from that angle."

"Well, it's the truth," Hank stated, still frowning. "I've never known a woman who didn't constantly nag at a man to change the way he dressed, the people he hung around with, the hobbies he enjoyed. Nag, nag, nag. And then they want you to go shopping with them. They start asking your opinion of their clothes, their jewelry and their hair. And watch out if you ever give the wrong answer! You'll be sleepin' in the dog-house for a week.''

Gwendolyn laughed at the picture he painted, which she was fairly certain was another McCauley exaggeration. ''Surely not everyone you know has this type of relationship.''

''Maybe not all of them, but from personal experience, I know I seem to attract that type of woman.''

What about me? The thought popped into Gwendolyn's head completely unexpected…and unwelcome, she told herself. She had not planned to audition for Hank McCauley's version of the perfect woman. The only man she wanted to please at the moment was King Wilheim, and she was fairly certain that wasn't going to happen.

''So what about you? Why haven't you found your own personal prince to keep you warm through those long winters?''

''That's a rather short, boring subject. I simply haven't had time.''

''You work day and night?''

''Not exactly, but my schedule doesn't permit much flexibility. I work erratic hours and I need to be on call for any emergencies.''

''With that damned prince, I can see how that could happen.''

''Really, he doesn't do things like this often.''

''If I ever have the misfortune to meet the guy, I'm likely to give him a piece of my mind—and maybe give him a taste of Texas justice.''

''I'm sure that won't be necessary.'' She definitely didn't want Hank and Alexi fighting. Besides the fact they were evenly matched, the reasons for conflict were too muddied to be settled with fists. The best solution was for Alexi to slip out of this country quietly after the press conference the king wanted, leaving no problems behind.

"I'm just warnin' you, darlin'. You'd better keep that prince away from me, especially if he's messed with Kerry Lynn's head."

"Could we change the subject? I thought we weren't going to talk about him any longer."

"You're right." The waitress brought their orders on platters she warned were very hot. Steam wafted the heady fragrance of beans, rice, peppers and various sauces from the food spread before them.

"This might be your last dinner in Texas," Hank said in a serious tone after she'd taken a bite. "I thought you should eat something authentic, in a down-home restaurant rather than one of those chains."

"Thank you. That's very thoughtful."

"And a little bit selfish," he admitted. "I wanted you to remember Texas…and me…with fondness. This trip hasn't been easy on you, I know, and you'd be justified if you wanted to put the whole fiasco out of your head. But we had some good times, too, and I'd like for you to remember those instead."

She leaned across the table and took his hand. "I will. I promise. I'll never forget the time I spent here with you."

He looked so serious, so unlike the Hank who usually smiled and teased his way through life. This Hank was a man with something on his mind, something weighty and intense.

She almost asked him about his feelings, but then decided to wait. Or maybe she'd never have the nerve.

Maybe she didn't want to know. She took a deep breath and looked away from his blue eyes.

The moment passed as she released his hand. They both returned their attention to their dinners, but Gwendolyn barely tasted the fragrant food. Her awareness was centered on Hank...and all the words left unsaid between them.

They drove back to his ranch at sunset. Gwendolyn admired the coral, pink and purple clouds, trying not to think about tonight, which must be her last with Hank. She simply couldn't tolerate another day, wondering how many more hours she'd have with him. Wondering if she'd be able to depart with her dignity intact. She had to choose the time of their parting rather than leaving it to fate. Tomorrow morning, whether or not the prince showed up, she was leaving Hank's ranch. She'd swallow her pride, reveal her deception to King Wilheim, and call the Texas authorities to find Alexi.

But tonight, Hank was still all hers.

The coast was clear as they parked Juan's pickup in front of the house. The dually was already in back of the house, out of sight of the road. While Gwendolyn walked into the dark house, Hank and Juan talked for a moment. A few minutes later she heard the crunch of gravel as Hank's worker drove away.

The quiet of the night pressed down on her as Hank shut and locked the door. His footsteps rang loud and clear as he walked across the tile floor toward her.

''Stay with me tonight,'' he said as he took her in his arms.

She couldn't speak, but nodded against his chest as her arms curled up his back. He was warm, solid and very real. Tonight he was all hers; tomorrow she would walk away from him, his ranch, and everything that had become dear to her in the past several days.

He bent his head and captured her lips, their tongues mating in a familiar yet exciting dance. He tasted of spicy Tex-Mex food and beer, a flavor she would always associate with her time with Hank, although she doubted she would ever sample that type of food again. The memories would be too strong, the emotions too overwhelming.

He skimmed his hands up her back, then deftly unfastened her bra beneath her cotton sweater. Gwendolyn sighed as he massaged the tightness from her muscles. She pulled his shirt free from his jeans and ran her hands along his spine, loving the feel of him beneath her fingers. No other man felt like Hank, so warm and solid. She wanted to taste him all over.

Without warning he scooped down, grabbed the back of her thighs and lifted her against his arousal. Gwendolyn gasped and wrapped her legs around his waist, silently blessing the skirt she'd worn today. She held tight as he began to walk out of the kitchen toward his bedroom. Toward the bed that had been so welcoming last night…and early this morning.

She ran her tongue along the column of his neck. "You taste good," she whispered into his ear.

Hank shuddered. "I'm probably sweaty."

"Salty," she replied. "I like salty."

He lowered her to the bed slowly, keeping her pressed against him, her legs locked around his waist. "You are so beautiful," he said, leaning down and spreading her hair across the pillow, "especially when your eyes get all dreamy and your lips part like you're just waiting for me to kiss you."

"I am waiting," she said softly. "Kiss me now."

"Still demanding," he replied with a smile. "Whatever my lady wants."

His lady. She could only wish that were true. Then he kissed her and she forgot to wish, forgot to think. He lowered himself onto the mattress and moved against her until she gasped.

"I want you naked," she whispered as she grabbed his shirt, then gave in to her urge and pulled the snaps apart. His hands were in the way, busy undressing her. Finally he had her bare to the waist. She pushed his shirt down his arms. The feel of his bare chest against her breasts was heavenly, but soon it wasn't enough.

They rolled away in unison, quickly removing the rest of their clothes, and then she was back in his arms. His mouth moved from her lips, down her neck and to her breast. As she gasped, his mouth closed around her nipple. The sensation was so wonderful that she moaned aloud.

"Love me," she gasped.

"Gwendolyn," he whispered against her damp, heated flesh, "what am I going to do without you?"

How could she answer such a question when she could barely remember her name? Then his lips trailed lower and she gasped again, grabbing the bed linens to keep from spinning off the mattress.

She couldn't stop touching him, running her hands over his hard body, memorizing every part of him. When he donned protection and joined his body with hers, the tears that she'd held in check slipped from her eyes. She moved with him, spiraling higher, flying beyond the limits of flesh and blood. With a cry she convulsed, holding him tight, feeling him surge one last time before he gasped her name and shuddered his completion.

She wasn't sure how many minutes passed until their breathing returned to normal. Eventually she became aware that the room was cool, the sheets were crisp, and she was holding Hank tight. She didn't want to let him go, she realized. Not tonight, not tomorrow.

As if he could read her mind, he whispered, "Stay with me tomorrow. For a week, or two weeks, or however long you can be away."

"I can't," she said against his chest. "I have to go back to my real life. To my career."

"Why?"

Because it's all I have. The answer popped into her head like a revelation from above. At the same time, she wanted to deny the truth. She was not some pitiful, aging career woman with no prospects. These were the best years of her life. She had a wonderful job, and most of the time she adored the people she worked with. Yes, her family didn't understand her need to succeed, but she had friends. She had a life in Belegovia and in England.

"People depend on me," she said carefully. "As soon as Prince Alexi decides on a bride, I'll need to help prepare her for the media onslaught. Then I'll work with the wedding planner to coordinate everything."

"Someone else's bride. Someone else's wedding."

"That's my job," she said softly.

"Stay," he said, propping himself on one elbow to look down at her.

"I can't," she whispered.

He looked at her for a long time, then leaned down and kissed her tenderly. "Then stay the night."

Gwendolyn nodded, framing his beloved face with her hands. "One more night."

THE PHONE WOKE THEM to predawn grayness. Hank jumped up from a night of intermittent sleep, punctuated with dreams of Gwendolyn walking away while he ran to catch her, but never gained any ground. He shook his head and reached for the receiver.

"This better be important."

"It is," the voice on the other end said in hushed tones.

"Kerry Lynn?" At his words, Gwendolyn stirred beside him and sat up, hugging the sheet to her breasts. "Where in the hell are you?"

"In the office of the Four Square Café. We're kind of trapped here."

"We? Is the prince with you?"

"Yes."

"Kerry Lynn, what were you thinking?"

He heard her sigh, then nothing. She must have placed her hand over the mouthpiece. In a moment she whispered fiercely, "Hank, don't start in on me. I'm not apologizing to you or anyone for what I did."

"That damned prince is more important than your family?"

"Look, my mother and my sisters will understand. They'll be there for me today and tomorrow and forever, but Alexi is leaving—"

"The sooner the better."

"Don't start in on him. I mean it, Hank. I didn't call you to hear the outraged older-brother routine, although you're darned good at it."

"I'm serious, Kerry. Do you have any idea how long we've been looking for the two of you? That damned prince is supposed to be touring Texas, kissing babies and eating with the governor!"

"First of all, his name is Alexi. Except sometimes

I call him Mack. And he's not a damned prince, he's a man who needed a break.''

"Without thinking of what he did to the rest of the world. Wendy has just about gone nuts trying to find him.''

"Wendy?''

"Er, Lady Gwendolyn Reed. Ask your boyfriend. He knows very well who she is.''

"Yes, he told me she'd handle everything.''

"With no help from him!'' Wendy placed a hand on his arm and shook her sleep-tousled hair. Hank swiveled his legs over the side of the bed and sat up. "Look, Kerry, we have a problem. There are tabloid reporters lurking around town. They've gotten the idea that the prince is having a torrid affair with a local girl—you.''

"Gee, ya think?'' she replied in that saucy tone that had always made him want to spank her bottom—in a very big-brotherly fashion. "Why do you imagine we've been hiding out in the apartment over the café all night?''

"All night?'' Hank frowned. He didn't like the sound of that. "I didn't even know there was an apartment up there.''

"Yes, and it's been empty for a long time. The point is, those reporters are staying at that little bed-and-breakfast that just opened on the other side of the square above Robin Parker's antique shop. For all we know, they could be watching the café as we speak.''

"Well, don't let them see you together!''

"I hadn't planned on it, you big goober. I don't think they know my car, so I'm hopeful we can make it out the back door, take the alley to the one-way street on the other side of the square, and circle around. The question is, where can we go?''

''They'll be watching your mother's house,'' Hank said thoughtfully. ''We need a neutral place, but I don't want to risk driving all over the countryside until we can meet up. Tell Alexi that Milos Anatole and the driver, Pete Boedecker, are at the Motel 6 in San Marcus.''

He heard Kerry talking, then she came back on the phone. ''We could meet someplace around here, then drive to San Marcus together and meet up with them. Is Lady Gwendolyn staying at the same motel?''

''Uh, no, she's not.'' Hank glanced behind him at Wendy's frowning, confused features. ''We decided it would be better if she were here at the house for when the prince showed up.''

''So go wake her up and tell her what's going on.''

''She's already up.''

Silence. ''Hank, is she right there?''

''None of your business, squirt.''

''So you can hand her the phone?''

''I can do that, but first we need to decide where to meet. How about behind the Kash 'n' Karry?''

''Too public,'' Kerry objected. ''Someone might be there early.''

''What about the old homestead on Travis's property? That's on the back way to San Marcus, and we can leave your car there.''

''Okay. When can you get there?''

He looked back at Wendy. ''Give us thirty minutes.''

''Okay,'' Kerry said with a sigh. ''Thanks, Hank.''

''That's okay, squirt. I know this wasn't your fault.''

"You don't know any such thing," she said before she disconnected the call.

"Damn," he said, rubbing his hand across his face. "This isn't the way I wanted to start the morning."

"Yes," Wendy said, rolling toward the other side of the bed. "But we knew this was coming."

He leaned back and captured her hand before she gathered her clothes and headed for the bathroom. "I wasn't ready for the morning to come so quickly," he confessed.

"But it was inevitable, wasn't it?" she answered softly. "The night is over." Taking a deep breath, she hugged her jeans and cotton sweater to her chest before escaping to the privacy of the guest bath off the hall.

Hank didn't want to hurry but knew they didn't have much time. He rushed through a shower and didn't bother to shave. Pulling on his jeans and a clean shirt, he thought about Wendy. She was probably plotting the switch, wording statements in her head and preparing plausible explanations for everything that the tabloid reporters thought they knew.

Would she have even a moment to think about last night? He hoped the hell she did. If he was going to be miserable, he wanted her to share some of his pain. He wanted to know she regretted their parting. He wanted her to feel the loss, like someone was slowly tearing off a limb or removing a vital organ.

He'd done the impossible; he'd fallen in love with exactly the wrong kind of woman at the worst possible moment.

Chapter Thirteen

Gwendolyn felt as though she hadn't seen Alexi in months rather than days. Just behind the house with faded white paint and aged wood, the crown prince of Belegovia and Hank's former girlfriend waited in the pale light of dawn. As the tires of Hank's dually crunched through knee-high weeds already turning brown in the late-spring heat, over the rutted path of gravel and dirt, she leaned forward in the seat for her first sign of the prince.

Yes, she wanted to shake him until his perfect teeth rattled. She wanted to yell at him like a fishwife, asking him what he was possibly thinking to run off like that. But she would do neither. She would hold her tongue and save her anger for later, when they were safely on the private jet back to Belegovia.

On the plane, flying away from Hank… She could barely imagine leaving so abruptly. Her stomach felt queasy as the truck swayed from side to side. Tension speared her neck and shoulders as the bumper of a pale blue car appeared behind the corner of a peeling red barn, shaded from the slanting rays of morning sun by a large tree.

"They're here," Hank said, his knuckles white as

he gripped the steering wheel. He frowned as fiercely and intensely as he did with everything. He could become angry just as quickly as he could laugh, and his moods might seem volatile to some people. But Gwendolyn knew Hank cared about those who were awarded with both his teasing and his frowns.

With one last look behind him to make sure he hadn't been followed, he turned behind the house and parked the dually beneath the large tree, next to the compact car.

Gwendolyn didn't wait for Hank to shut off the engine; she opened her door and jumped down from the truck. Alexi stood with his arms draped around the petite blond waitress Gwendolyn had met at the truck stop a lifetime ago.

"I had planned to save my lecture for later, when we were alone, but I cannot hold my tongue," she announced as she strode toward the couple. "Of all the irresponsible stunts you've pulled over the years, Alexi Ladislas, this one is the worst, do you hear me?" she hissed as she stood in front of the somber couple. Her voice rose to a screech. "What were you thinking?"

"Hello, Gwendolyn," the prince responded calmly to her theatrics. "You remember Kerry, don't you?" He looked beyond, his gaze dark. "I don't believe I've had the pleasure of meeting my alter ego."

"I'm not your alter ego, you inconsiderate son of a—"

"Hank!" Gwendolyn took one look at his clenched fists and grabbed his arm before he marched right up to Alexi and punched his nose.

"You don't think much of me, I know. Well, we don't have time to go into our differences at the moment,'' Alexi said calmly, rubbing his hand up and down Kerry Lynn's arm. The young blonde looked as though she was trying to be poised in the face of two irrational combatants and a supreme diplomat. ''The truth is, I can't completely explain my actions.'' He looked down at Kerry with such a tender expression that Gwendolyn's breath caught in her throat. *My God, he's in love with her.* She closed her mouth and stared.

''Kerry Lynn, are you okay?'' Hank asked, shaking off Gwendolyn's hand.

''Of course I'm okay,'' Kerry said, raising her chin and glaring at him. ''Now, try to be nice while we drive to San Marcus, will you? If you'd give Alex a chance, you'd like him.''

''Fat chance. He's caused too many people too much trouble for me to be civil to the guy.''

''Hank, please,'' Gwendolyn said, placing her hand on his arm again. ''I know you're angry, but Kerry's right. We don't have time for arguments. We must get our stories straight. I've decided we're going to have a 'meeting' of the two of you later today, so you have one more acting challenge in front of you.''

He looked down at her, his expression fierce. ''I'm doin' this for you, not for him,'' he said, jerking his thumb in the direction of the prince. ''For all I care, he can dig himself out of the mess he's made.''

''Oh, that's just great, Hank McCauley,'' Kerry Lynn said, pulling away from Alexi and glaring at the cowboy. ''You know what? This isn't about you. I don't want my mother and sisters to read tacky comments and downright lies about me in the papers. If you care anything at all about me, you won't make me go through that.''

''Dammit, Kerry, you should have thought of that

before you ran off with the guy,'' Hank said, shaking his finger at her. "If you were a few years younger, I'd turn you over my knee and blister your bottom."

"You'd do no such thing, you big fraud. Now, quit trying to sound so fierce and calm down. We don't have that much time left,'' she said, looking up at Alexi with longing.

"Yes, let's be off,'' Gwendolyn said before more harsh words could be exchanged. "We must work out the details so there won't be any lapses in front of the cameras or microphones.''

"All right,'' Hank said, sounding like a little boy whose toys had been temporarily taken away, "but I'd better be hearin' an apology to Lady Wendy for all the problems your runaway prince has caused.''

"He's not my—'' Kerry started to say.

"Gwendolyn, I truly am sorry for the problems my impulsive actions caused,'' Alexi said. He looked as though he wanted to take her hand, as he often did when he was being sincere and charming, but Hank's venomous glare stopped him.

Hank McCauley was one of the few people in the world who had the ability to make Prince Alexi of Belegovia back down. The sight was awe-inspiring, Gwendolyn thought as she glanced from one man to the other. Yes, they looked alike in a superficial manner, but they were worlds apart in disposition, background and goals.

Suddenly, Gwendolyn realized what had been eluding her since she'd met Hank. The main difference was that Hank knew what he wanted from life: his ranch, training horses and living among friends he cared for and who cared for him. Alexi, on the other hand, despite being a prince and heir to a monarchy, hadn't yet found his own personal goal. His random and occasional outbursts of irresponsibility were his way of seeking a personal life, separate from the royal family.

Her anger deflated. She reached forward and took Alexi's hand as she hadn't done in years, since they were school chums back in England. "I understand, truly I do. And I'm sorry for yelling at you."

"Wendy, don't start apologizing. You had a right to be angry," Hank said indignantly.

"Yes, I did. And now I have a right to accept his apology and get on with things. Come along, then. We have a lot to accomplish and only about half an hour before we meet Milos and Mr. Boedecker."

The men stared at her as though she'd gone daft, but she didn't have time to explain her revelations.

"Great idea. Come on, guys," Kerry Lynn said, tugging the prince toward the pickup truck. "I'll bet you've never ridden in the back seat of a dually."

He gazed fondly at her. "No, I haven't."

Gwendolyn watched Hank glare at their retreating backs. "Please, try to be considerate," she said. "I think your anger at Prince Alexi may hurt Kerry Lynn more than help her."

Hank turned to face her, still frowning. "Is that what you think this is about? Kerry?" He shook his head. "I'm madder than a wet hen because of the way he treated *you*, not Kerry."

"I'm fine, really."

"You deserve more than his irresponsible actions and a halfway sincere apology."

"He truly is sorry, Hank. I've known him for years, and believe me, I can tell more about what he's thinking and feeling than you."

"So that's supposed to reassure me?"

"No, I'm just explaining. Alexi and I are old friends, much like you and Kerry. I care for him as a friend, and yes, he's hurt my feelings before. I'll get over it." She swallowed and put on her best professional smile to hide the fact her heart was ripping in two. "What I won't be able to forget is your anger. I don't want to part like this."

He looked at her blankly a moment, as though her words made no sense. "You're not gone yet."

"No, but I will be. Things will progress rapidly today, and I'm afraid we won't have time alone."

"Wendy, don't—" He reached for her, but she headed for the truck.

"And we will need to keep to a strict schedule to assure the press the prince is recovering from his cold, and you and Kerry were together all along, and you've just met the prince when the two of you shake hands for the photographers."

"Don't leave like this. We need more time."

"I'm sorry," she said as she kept on walking, unshed tears burning her eyes, "but our time has run out."

HANK COOLED HIS HEELS at the Dairy Queen in San Marcus with Kerry Lynn while the prince showered, shaved and dressed in his designer clothes. He was bound to look different than he had this morning, when they'd met up behind the barn. Hank had the strangest feeling he was looking in a mirror, seeing the prince dressed in jeans and a white shirt, the sleeves rolled up, with his arm around Kerry Lynn.

"How much longer?" she asked after taking a long sip of her Oreo Blizzard.

Hank glanced at his watch. "Five minutes." He ran his hand over his bristly jaw. "I sure wish Wendy would have let me shave. I feel like the back end of a porcupine."

"The scruffy look makes you seem different from the prince."

"I know, but I'd be a heck of a lot more comfortable in clean clothes and no beard."

"We've had a wild weekend, remember? You're not supposed to look well groomed."

He looked at her long and hard, like he would a sister who'd spent four days with some guy she'd just met. "Is that what you and the prince had—a wild weekend?"

"None of your business," she said, slurping the last mouthful of Blizzard from the cup.

"What does your momma think about all this?"

Kerry suddenly looked uncomfortable. "We haven't had time to talk. She'd already left when I took Alexi by the café. You know I didn't see her after the graduation ceremony, mainly because I knew you would find me and I'd have to explain everything. I didn't want to get into all that in the crowd."

"She was worried about you when I went to see her at the Four Square Café Friday."

"I'm a grown woman, Hank, not some silly teenager. I've worked damn hard the past ten years and I deserved this short vacation."

"Is that all it was?"

She sat her empty cup in the drink holder, her expression pained. "That's all it can be, Hank. He's a *prince.* Do you realize how far apart we are in every way that matters?"

He gripped the steering wheel to keep his fists from clenching. "Yeah, I guess I do."

Kerry looked up at him with those big green eyes of hers. "Because of you and Lady Gwendolyn?"

He took a deep breath and looked away. "I suppose. But like you said, we're worlds apart."

"Maybe she'd stay if you asked real nice."

"I asked. She wasn't buying."

"I'm sorry. Maybe it's for the best, though. I mean, she's an English lady and she's used to the life she has at the palace in Belegovia and in those drafty old manor houses back home. She'd probably last a month in Texas before she went running back to Europe."

"Yeah, you're probably right." But he sure as hell would have liked a chance to find out.

They sat in silence for a moment, then Hank reached for the keys and cranked the engine. "Let's get going. Sittin' in the Dairy Queen and commiserating on our troubles is too depressin'."

"Yeah, you're right. Let's get this show on the road."

He pulled the dually out of the parking space and headed back to Ranger Springs.

His greatest acting challenge hadn't been convincing the governor of Texas that he was a foreign prince, nor had it been pretending to converse with an Italian contessa. No, his greatest acting challenge would be to hide the fact he was in love with Lady Gwendolyn Reed.

THE GAZEBO ON THE TOWN square in Ranger Springs was draped in red, white and blue crepe paper. The Fourth of July Festival committee had been pressed into service early this year, stapling and taping the annual decorations in place in the middle of May. A microphone had been positioned inside the gazebo for speaking to the crowd of citizens and reporters who had gathered. On one of the benches inside the gazebo, Travis's friend and neighbor, Hank McCauley, sat beside Kerry Lynn Jacks, who didn't look real happy to be here this afternoon. Hank looked kind of scruffy, as though he'd just gotten out of bed, which was strange. Hank never appeared in public without a good close shave. Something odd was happening here besides a royal visit.

Frankly, Travis thought as he gazed out at the audience, there were more reporters than curious spectators. He hadn't seen that many cameras since he'd taken his niece and nephew to Disney World. There were two news crews with video equipment, one from San Antonio and one from Austin. He suspected there would have been more except for the hurried nature of this visit.

Mrs. Jacks stood nervously near the entrance to the gazebo. Dr. Ambrose Wheatley and his wife Joyce stood beside her, and Thelma Rogers tested her own voice into a black cassette recorder she held in one hand.

Police Chief Ethan Parker looked very official despite the fact his wife Robin leaned against him. Dr. Amy Wheatley walked over and began a conversation, and Ethan laughed. Grayson Phillips, Dr. Amy's husband, walked over from his silver Lexus and joined the group.

Travis was glad he didn't have a woman leaning on him, although he had to admit that everyone looked very happy. Still, some men were cut out for happily ever after, and some weren't. He'd tried and failed; he wasn't ready to get tied down again.

Just when he was getting real restless, thinking about all the couples surrounding him, a buzz started in the crowd. A black Land Rover drove up, the tinted windows making it difficult to see who was sitting in the back seat. Judging from the snap of the cameras, there wasn't any doubt—this was the prince of Belegovia and his entourage.

Paparazzi rushed forward, crowding against the thin barrier of rope strung up to make a walkway from the curb to the gazebo. Ethan Parker's two patrol officers stood nearby, ready for crowd control, just in case any of the European photojournalists got too pushy.

A real pretty, real classy lady got out of the left side of the Land Rover's back seat. She wore a dark suit and black pumps. A small man, a real spiffy-looking guy who looked like he might be a butler, got out of the front. Then the other back door opened and the man everyone had come to see stepped onto the concrete sidewalk of Ranger Springs, Texas. Dressed in a dark suit, red tie and shiny Italian shoes, he looked like a model for *GQ*.

Travis glanced over at Mrs. Jacks. She looked like she might faint at any minute. Maybe he ought to stand beside her, just in case. The woman had a serious case of royal fascination. He pushed his way through the crowd as Prince Alexi walked in front of his entourage toward the gazebo.

He was a good-looking man. Of course, he could have been Hank's twin, so he was bound to be handsome as the devil. He didn't have Hank's laughing eyes and easygoing grin, though. This man looked tall, lean and powerful in every sense, as if he knew he'd been born to money and position. Which, of course, he had.

The prince stopped in front of the mayor and city leaders, shaking hands and speaking softly while the cameras continued to click away. The citizens of Ranger Springs had joined in with their disposable cameras, ancient 35 millimeters, and even a few Polaroids. The next-day photo service at the drugstore was going to be real busy tomorrow.

Travis glanced up at Hank and found him standing, grim-faced, beside a nervous Kerry Lynn. Nervous? Why in the world would she be nervous? Travis seriously doubted meeting a prince, even one as single and handsome as Alexi Ladislas, would cause concern from the feisty waitress. And why wasn't Hank putting on his good ol' boy charm? Something was seriously wrong here, but now wasn't the time to ask.

Finally, the prince made his way up the steps to the gazebo. Hank stepped forward and shoved his hand at the visiting dignitary. The prince smiled and clasped it. Travis got the impression the two men were each trying to crush the other's hand. Again, he couldn't figure out why. They finally parted and Kerry Lynn stepped forward, extending her hand. Damn, she looked like she was going to cry. Instead of shaking her hand, the prince leaned forward and kissed first one cheek, then the other, in the European manner. He seemed to linger a little too long, though, and Kerry Lynn's eyes got all misty.

Was the prince putting the moves on Kerry Lynn, right in front of Hank? And why was Kerry Lynn with Hank if he'd been off with another woman for four days? None of this made any sense.

The natty little man stood to one side, but the good-looking classy woman stepped forward. She stood straight and fairly tall. With brisk movements she extended her hand, first to Hank, then to Kerry. Hank looked tense enough to chew nails.

Something strange was happening inside that gazebo.

The mayor stepped up to the microphone and droned on about how happy everyone was to welcome visiting royalty. He then introduced Lady Gwendolyn Reed, public relations director for the monarchy of Belegovia.

The tall woman advanced up to the microphone. She looked real professional, but a little tense also.

"Good afternoon. Thank you for coming today to our impromptu trip to the heart of the Texas Hill Country." Her accent was British upper class rather than European.

A murmur of excitement and approval swept through the crowd before she continued. "As you may know, Prince Alexi of Belegovia has been on a visit to your wonderful state. Unfortunately, he has suffered from laryngitis and a cold during the last few days. His doctor recommended he rest his voice and recuperate at the hotel in Austin. During this time, certain unprofessional journalists erroneously reported that the prince was not in his hotel room."

Another murmur went through the crowd. Even Travis knew about the tabloid story that had stated that the prince was having a torrid affair with a Texas gold-digger. A grainy photo of Hank and Kerry Lynn, taken off some Internet Web site, had appeared with the story, along with more recent photos of Hank going into the Four Square Café, looking a bit shifty.

"In addition to visiting this lovely town, the prince

would like to take this opportunity to set the record straight. It is my privilege to introduce His Highness, Prince Alexi of Belegovia.''

A round of applause and a few whistles went up from the crowd. The cameras started clicking again. Mrs. Jacks looked real pale. Travis put one hand under her elbow just in case she decided to pass out on the grass.

''Thank you,'' the prince said, putting up his hands to stop the applause. He smiled, flashing white teeth and a winning grin. ''I am very happy to be with you today,'' he said, his voice still raspy. He placed a hand on his throat. ''I hope you don't have any trouble understanding me because I truly am hoarse.''

The crowd applauded. The prince smiled, then continued. ''We are often plagued by rumors and false reports from certain disreputable journalists. As a member of the royal family, I have learned to tolerate this. However, the tabloids have now involved an innocent young woman, and this I will not tolerate.''

A huge cheer went up from the crowd of spectators. The professional photojournalists continued to click away. ''I have just met a man who looks enough like me to be my twin, Mr. Hank McCauley. Also, I have learned that Miss Kerry Lynn Jacks, who is a friend of Mr. McCauley, has recently returned to town from a trip to visit relatives.''

Although his voice seemed to have lost the hoarseness he'd begun with, he seemed to have a sudden relapse. When he began speaking again, he sounded more gravelly. ''As you can see, the resemblance between myself and Mr. McCauley has led to some unfortunate speculation from the media. I sincerely regret the inference that Miss Jacks is involved.''

Suddenly, everything made sense. Hank leaving the ranch. The prince getting laryngitis. The tabloid reports.

Another big cheer rang out. Prince Alexi had obviously won the hearts of the Texans watching. As Travis glanced at Kerry Lynn, he got the distinct impression he might have won her heart, too. When he looked at Hank, he saw a man hurting…and watching the pretty, classy English lady like she was tearing him apart.

Chapter Fourteen

Gwendolyn felt emotionally and physically drained as she walked from the gazebo to the Four Square Café for a small, private reception. She wasn't sure who would attend, but she hoped a minimum amount of people would witness her pathetic attempt to hold herself together. *Just a few hours until we board the jet for Belegovia,* she told herself. *I can keep it together that long.*

Hank held the door open for Kerry and her as the bell tinkled merrily. His scent filled her with longing. She wanted to turn to him, bury her nose against his chest and feel his strong arms closing around her.

Well, perhaps she might not maintain her composure as long as he was watching her. He'd looked at her throughout the brief press event as though he expected her to confess everything to the reporters and spectators. And to what end? The truth would hurt all those affected, especially King Wilheim, and couldn't serve any useful purpose.

Her feelings for Hank had nothing to do with the truth or the deception. Confessing that she cared far too much for the Texas cowboy wouldn't change the circumstances of their lives. He was so firmly established here, so confident and well liked, and she was still hoping to find her way in the complicated world of family and career.

"Thank you," she murmured as she slipped past Hank into the cheerful café.

A punch bowl had been set up in the middle of the room, surrounded by assorted cookies and cakes, while coffee service and iced tea lined the walls. The chrome-and-gray Formica tables had been polished until they glowed, and shiny red vinyl booths lined the back walls on either side of a wide, open window to the kitchen.

The Ranger Springs dignitaries were all beaming. Unlike their more sophisticated counterparts in Austin, the civic leaders weren't ashamed to be caught admiring the prince, basking in his presence. Gwendolyn smiled in spite of her personal pain. She found these Texans refreshing and very real, and wished she had more time to know them. Hank had said they were good people, and she had to agree.

"We need to talk," Hank whispered in her ear as he walked up behind her.

"I can hardly leave the reception."

"You can slip away for a few minutes," he replied softly. "Kerry tells me there's an apartment upstairs. Pretend you're going to the ladies' room and come up the steps in back of the kitchen."

"Hank, I don't think—"

"I'll expect you in ten minutes. You owe me."

"For pretending to be the prince?"

He looked at her blankly, then his expression hardened, his blue eyes frosty. "Yeah, that's right. We never did decide on my fee, did we?"

"Whatever you think is fair," she said tonelessly.

She'd promised to pay him for his time, and he'd gone way beyond the call of duty. She just hadn't expected to pay with her heart.

"Be there or I'll drag you somewhere private. We *are* gonna talk before you leave."

Hank walked away, escorting Kerry Lynn to where her mother stood with a few other Ranger Springs citizens. From across the room, Gwendolyn watched Alexi charm them all. She looked at Kerry as the young woman turned to gaze at the prince.

Gwendolyn wondered if the truck-stop waitress and recent college graduate knew that her heart was in her eyes.

A young woman with glowing skin and honey-blond hair brought her a cup of punch. "I hope you've had a good visit to Texas," she said in a very un-Texas accent. "I'm Robin Parker, wife of the chief of police. I also run the antique shop and bed and breakfast across the town square," she said, nodding toward a building that sported a marquee similar to a movie theater.

"Thank you. The trip has been very educational," Gwendolyn replied. In fact, she'd learned she could fall in love and have her heart broken by circumstances beyond her control in only five days. "I'll never forget my visit to Texas."

"That's wonderful. We're very glad you decided to visit Ranger Springs, even though the circumstances were unfortunate. Those tabloid reporters will print anything, won't they?"

"They can be very creative."

A few more people walked up and chatted, each one of them expressing their regret she and the prince had been brought to their town due to tabloid reporters and paparazzi. As quickly as possible, Gwendolyn excused herself and walked toward the back of the restaurant. She dreaded seeing Hank alone, but a part of her wanted to be with him one more time.

Checking to make sure she wasn't followed, she slipped past the rest rooms and through a door marked Kitchen. The area was silent, filled with the smells of grease and disinfectant. In the back, the staircase awaited.

She paused, reminding herself she did owe Hank one more conversation. Belegovia also owed him a great debt. She had to face him, hear what he had to say and make whatever amends she could.

Still, her feet would not climb the stairs quickly or cheerfully.

"Hank?" she called out.

"In here."

She followed the sound of his voice to a living room. Late-afternoon sunlight entered through two windows overlooking the town square. Hank sprawled on a nubby beige sofa, his expression unreadable.

Gwendolyn took the only other seat, a rocking chair, and drew in a deep breath. "We shouldn't be gone from the reception for very long."

"I know you'd rather fly out of here without talking about what happened between us, but I can't let that happen."

Gwendolyn shook her head, but he continued. "We haven't known each other long, but we have something special. I think you can admit that."

"Yes, but—"

"And I don't understand how you can think that going back to Belegovia will change how we feel."

She hadn't thought about her feelings from that

angle. Would she feel differently about Hank when she was in her small apartment at the royal palace?

"Perhaps our feelings won't change, but what do you expect us to do? We live in two different worlds. We're at two different points in our lives. You're so settled, so together." She shrugged. "I'm still trying to prove myself in my career. I can't just run out on my goals."

Hank rose off the couch in one fluid motion and stepped in front of her. "Darlin', I think you just hit the nail on the head. You're trying to prove yourself. To whom? Prince Alexi? I don't think so, since it's obvious he admires and respects you. The king? Maybe, but I've got to ask if maybe he's more like another father to you. And that brings me to your own daddy. What are you trying to prove to him?"

"That's…that's silly. The king is not another father, and my father doesn't even believe I should have a career."

"Exactly. What better way to show him you're worthy of his respect than to succeed? He's bound to know that you're doing a good job for the royal family in Belegovia. I'll bet the tape from that little news conference you arranged on the spur of the moment gets picked up by CNN and the BBC by tomorrow morning."

"Perhaps, but my father will probably say that a man could have done the job better, or he'll remind me that even though I'm doing a good job, I could be an even better wife to one of his peers."

"Then he's a fool," Hank said, kneeling beside her chair. "You're a wonderful, competent woman. You're not some commodity to be purchased by the guy with the biggest title."

"Thank you," she said softly. "I'm glad you understand what I've been trying to tell my father for ages."

He reached for her hands. "Now I'm gonna tell you something, darlin'. You can't live your life tryin' to please your daddy or impress your family. I learned early on in my career that it doesn't matter how many buckles you win or how much money you've stacked up in the bank if you're not the kind of person that people admire. Wendy, you've already proved your worth time and again by the way people feel about you. You're kind and sweet, caring and intelligent. You take care of people all the way through, from their feelings to their comfort. You give a lot to everyone and don't expect a thing for yourself. All you want is the approval of someone who may never understand or admire your accomplishments."

She shook her head. "I'm not some saint. I make lots of mistakes and I'm often petty. Just today I got angry at Alexi."

"Yeah, and you kept me from punching his lights out," Hank said with a grin. "I think that was pretty charitable of you, considering his actions, but I won't go into that again." His grin faded as he continued. "My point is that you deserve to go after what you want. I'm not braggin', darlin', but I think you want me."

He'd never know how much she wanted him. Desperately. Completely. "We're worlds apart."

"We have more in common than we'd ever imagined. Most of all, we have the same values. And you like my ranch, I know you do. I've seen it in your eyes when you gaze at the wildflowers, swim in the pool or just watch the clouds float across the sky.

You're great on horseback, even if you are used to those little saddles."

"This isn't all about me, Hank. You can't possibly believe we know enough about each other in five days to turn our lives upside down."

"Darlin', I believe we know enough about each other to spend the rest of our lives together. I don't give a damn how long it took."

"Hank, no! You can't be sure—"

"I'm sure. I just don't understand why you won't admit that you are, too."

She jumped up from the rocker. "I don't know!"

"Listen to your heart. Inside, you know we love each other." He followed her across the room to the windows, placing his hands on her shoulders. "I know exactly how I feel. I love you, Gwendolyn."

"I can't fall in love with you. I barely know you. I've planned my career for years. I've known the importance of staying focused for as long as I can remember."

"Then maybe you should change your focus to *us.*"

She spun around, her heart pounding, her head spinning. Hank had never appeared more handsome, more appealing than he did at this moment. His blue eyes blazed, his sun-streaked hair fell over his forehead, and the stubble covering his jaw made him look a little wild and dangerous.

She didn't want sexy and dangerous. She wanted her career. She wanted her family to admit she'd done a great job. She wanted her father to admit he was wrong all along.

"I can't," she whispered.

"You're afraid."

Maybe. She'd never know, because she wasn't going to take the risk. She wasn't going to give up everything for the love of a cowboy she'd known for five days.

Instead, she leaned forward and pressed her lips to his. His mouth parted and he deepened the kiss. He put his heart and soul into kissing her, as if he could convince her that he was right. All she had to do was give in. Simply give up her life, her career, for a chance at happiness here in Texas.

That was easy for him. He wasn't giving up anything. If their relationship didn't work, he'd simply continue training his horses and visiting his friends. She would be the outsider, starting over and still trying to find where she belonged.

She pulled away, placing her hands on his chest. ''I can't,'' she whispered, and then she ran. Across the room. Down the steps. Her footsteps echoed on the high ceilings and haunted her as she ran for the safety of the reception below.

HANK KNEW HE SHOULD GO below, smile and chitchat with his friends and neighbors, but the effort seemed beyond him. Since early this morning when he'd gotten the phone call from Kerry Lynn, he'd been trying to get Wendy alone. He'd been so sure he could convince her to stay. They had something special, something he'd just recognized as love. He'd never really been in love before, so he didn't know what the overpowering sensations meant. He'd been attracted to her from the beginning, but now that he knew her, she made his heart sing and his spirits soar. They were good together; they should have a chance at a future.

But Wendy was scared. Frightened they'd only known each other for a few days. Worried about her career, and what leaving might signal to others. And she desperately, hopelessly, wanted to prove her worth to her worthless father.

Hank didn't know how he'd compete with her need to show the men in her family that she was talented, smart and skilled. If the jerks didn't get it, what more could she do? Dammit, she'd spend the next twenty years trying to prove she was good enough to be an equal with those British male chauvinists.

He wanted to be angry with her for not seeing the futility of the situation, but he couldn't. Not when she was so upset. Not when she was so torn by her desires to be with him and succeed in her career as Belegovia's royal public relations director.

And she had that damned wedding of that damned prince, Hank recalled, kicking the couch for good measure.

With a disgusted shake of his head, he paced across the room to the stairs. Everything was silent back in the kitchen. He could slip outside, get in his truck and drive away. Or he could go downstairs, see Wendy one more time, and have his heart shredded to ribbons by the sadness in her whiskey eyes.

There was no choice. He descended the steps, then pushed through the back door of the Four Square Café like the hounds of hell were chasing him. He'd done everything he could think of—besides kidnapping Wendy and holding her at his ranch until she came to her senses—and he'd failed to convince her. The next move was up to her.

Of course, he thought as he opened the door of the dually, he could always kidnap her later. He'd never been to Belegovia, but he was sure he could find the royal palace.

GWENDOLYN HID IN THE office of the Four Square Café until she stopped crying. She wished she had the small cosmetics bag she carried inside her purse, but she'd settled for some wet paper towels to soothe her puffy, red eyes. She couldn't do anything about the sadness she knew showed on her face, the same sadness that was eating her up. She'd just try to pretend she wasn't dying inside.

She gathered the wet paper towels and decided to make one more stop in the ladies' room. Perhaps someone else would be there. She might borrow some powder and lipstick to hide her blotchy complexion and pale, drawn mouth. She'd never cried prettily.

Pushing open the door to the small loo, she stopped and stared. Kerry Lynn Jacks stood at the washbasin, her own red-rimmed eyes and trembling lip telling Gwendolyn everything she needed to know about the young woman's feelings. Love seemed to be as contagious as colds in Texas.

"Does he know?" she asked gently.

Kerry shook her head, her fine blond hair flying. "We had a good time but it's over."

Gwendolyn took a deep breath and stepped closer, shutting the door and turning the lock to keep prying eyes outside. "Perhaps it's not that simple."

"I'm a former truck-stop waitress from Ranger Springs, Texas. He's the crown prince of an old, respected European country. What could be more simple than that?"

Kerry was right, of course. There was no future for her and the prince, even if they were in love. Or *thought* they were in love. How could they possibly know after only a few days together?

Or even if they were sure, how could they possibly

think it would work? People didn't know if they were compatible from such bizarre circumstances as the last five days. Learning about each other took months, possibly years.

But Gwendolyn was sure how she felt at the moment, even without any dreams of a happily-ever-after future.

"I'm very fond of your Hank McCauley."

"I figured as much from the way he was watching you. He sure never looked at me like that—which is fine," she added quickly. "Hank and I are more like cousins than anything romantic."

Gwendolyn smiled weakly and blotted her eyes once again. "He said brother and sister."

Kerry tried to smile back. "That's Hank. He's very responsible and the nicest guy I know."

Gwendolyn nodded. Yes, he was, but she wasn't looking for a nice man. A responsible man. Or any man at all. If she ran out on her job responsibilities right now, she'd prove that she wasn't capable. She might as well go back to England and find some titled bore who wanted an heir and a spare, a kennel full of hounds and a stable full of horses.

"We must go back outside and face everyone," Gwendolyn said. "Did you by chance bring your purse?"

Kerry nodded, holding up a striped canvas bag that looked full of promise.

"May I borrow some war paint, please? I'm going to need every advantage I can muster to get through the next hour."

Kerry handed her a clear vinyl bag brimming with cosmetics. "Are you leaving that soon?" she asked in a small voice.

"As quickly as possible. I think that would be best."

Kerry nodded, her eyes swimming with tears once more.

Gwendolyn placed the vinyl bag on the counter and put her arms around the woman who had the misfortune to love a prince. "We're a fine pair, aren't we?" Kerry said, her voice muffled by the padded shoulder of Gwendolyn's suit.

"Yes, we are." Two women who had nothing in common—except loving the wrong men.

SOMEHOW, GWENDOLYN GOT through the remainder of the small reception. She and Kerry returned and tried to smile, but she assumed they weren't successful in fooling anyone into believing they were happy and carefree. Several people looked concerned, especially Kerry's mother, Charlene Jacks. Gwendolyn steered the conversation away from anything personal when she was asked if she was "fine."

Of course I'm not fine, she wanted to say. Actually, she wanted to run out the door screaming, but since the paparazzi and photojournalists were still occupying the town square, she thought that might not be a good idea. Not when she was the model of decorum.

When she couldn't stand the tension a moment longer, she went to the prince and whispered in his ear, "We need to depart now."

He looked down at her, then across the room at Kerry. Gwendolyn knew how he felt; he wanted a moment alone with the young woman.

"I'll have the Land Rover brought around to the back. Then I'll take Kerry upstairs. Give me just a moment, then you can say goodbye." She paused and looked up into his eyes, which no longer seemed so blue, so like Hank's. He also didn't have that endearing little scar just above his upper lip. "You'll only have a few minutes, though."

Alexi nodded, then turned and smiled to the mayor. Gwendolyn walked quickly to Pete Boedecker, who was sitting with Milos Anatole at the table next to the front door. "Bring the car around back, please, and be ready to depart in five minutes."

Smiling to several people she had met earlier, she swept around the room and took Kerry Lynn's arm. "Can I see you for a moment?" she asked. Nodding to Mrs. Jacks, Gwendolyn steered Kerry toward the stairs.

"Alexi will be here in a moment. You'll have just five minutes. I'm sorry, but we need to leave."

"I understand."

Gwendolyn couldn't think of anything else to say, so she left the young woman alone and returned to the reception, nodding to Alexi. To cover up his departure from the room, she launched into an invitation for all the Ranger Springs residents to come and visit them in Belegovia, mentioning the winter skiing in the mountainous western part of the country and the quaint villages and shops in the rolling hillsides. She assured them that there were both modern and historic hotels, plus a newly renovated airport. The lively, animated conversation used up the rest of her reserves of strength, however, and when she saw Milos enter at the back and nod, she gave a silent prayer of thanks that the reception—and the deception—was over.

Alexi entered, charming as always, but his eyes appeared dark and troubled. He quickly said goodbye, shook more hands and swept out the back of the restaurant. If he'd lived two hundred years ago, he would have had a billowing cape following in his wake. Now he left with ringing footsteps and the sighs of those who had been impressed by His Royal Highness.

Within moments they were settled inside the Land Rover. Gwendolyn's head pounded as she closed her eyes and collapsed against the seat. "That was the hardest thing I've ever done," she whispered as they pulled out onto the street.

"Covering up my transgression or leaving Hank McCauley?" the prince asked.

She turned her head to glare at him, all pretense of employer-employee gone. "If you hadn't run off, I wouldn't have found it necessary to involve Mr. McCauley," she stated as they drove by the town square on their way out of town.

"Then you might never have met him, would you? I think you should be thanking rather than scolding me."

"Of all the arrogant... How can you possible make that statement?"

"Because you're in love with him," Alexi said simply.

Chapter Fifteen

"Don't be ridiculous," she denied after she regained her breath. "I can't possibly be in love with someone I just met."

Alexi leaned forward. "Milos, Mr. Boedecker, we're going to have a personal conversation now. Would you mind turning on the radio and listening to it rather than anything coming from the back seat?"

"Yes, Your Highness," Milos replied, switching on a country-western station she was sure had been Pete Boedecker's choice when he was alone.

Alexi turned his attention back to her as someone sang about broken hearts. "A week ago I would have agreed with you. Right now, I'm not so sure."

"Oh, Alexi," she said, placing a hand on his arm. He was so tense he felt like he was carved of wood. "I know about you and Kerry."

His head whipped around. "What do you know?"

Gwendolyn leaned close and whispered. "That she believes she's in love with you...and that you may feel the same way."

He slumped back against the seat. "She's an exceptional person, but I wouldn't characterize our relationship that way. I only wish..."

"What?"

"Never mind. I shouldn't have run away. I'm sorry, Gwendolyn. If I'd stayed with the schedule, none of this would have happened. We would have continued on with our merry lives, never knowing the pain of leaving so much unfinished."

"Yes. That would have been better, wouldn't it?"

He looked at her for a long time, then closed his eyes. "No."

She leaned back against her seat. "I didn't think so, either."

They drove in silence for a few minutes. When they were on the state highway again with no paparazzi following, Alexi straightened and said, "You distracted me, but you're not going to get off that easily. I want to know why you're here with me when you're obviously in love with Hank McCauley."

She stared at him, unable to answer that question without arguing her point...or stammering like a fool.

He narrowed his eyes, and for a moment, he looked so much like Hank she nearly cried. "Don't tell me he doesn't return your feelings. I saw the way he watched you during the press conference and when the reception first began...before he dragged you upstairs."

"Must I talk about my personal life? I can't imagine why you'd want to know about this since there is obviously no hope for a relationship."

"I don't know why you'd think that."

"Just like you and Kerry, there is no future for the two of us. We're from two different worlds, and we really don't know each other that well."

"You seemed to know enough about him to fall in love."

"Falling and staying are two different things," she said. "Besides, I never admitted how I feel."

"To him or to me? Because I believe either one of us can clearly see your emotions."

"Alexi, I really don't want to talk about this."

"That's because you know I'm right. There is no reason you can't go after your cowboy."

"There are a half-dozen reasons why pursuing a relationship would be futile."

"Gwendolyn, I know you come from an old family and your father places a lot of importance on your ability to breed the next generation of little English aristocrats, but you are *not* royalty. There is no reason why you can't have anyone you'd like. If you want Hank McCauley, go for it, as they say here in the States."

He paused, staring out the window as the countryside sped past. "Believe me, if I didn't need to marry someone suitable… Well, my life would be a lot different."

"I know, Alexi. We met the Contessa di Giovanni in Austin, you know. She's quite lovely."

"I've talked to my father. He's certain she'd make a perfect princess."

"He's probably right."

"I don't want a perfect princess, but I suppose that's exactly what I'll get."

Gwendolyn was afraid she knew what he wanted… a feisty Texas blond-haired, green-eyed waitress. "When you decide to marry, I'll be very busy coordinating the wedding. The marriage will be a media event unlike any we've seen since the last Monaco nuptials."

"If you had any sense, you'd be planning your own wedding."

"Don't be absurd. May I remind you *yet again* that I've only known Hank for five days, and under some very stressful situations. We were thrown together and had a similar goal. Naturally we had some...bonding. However, we are nothing alike."

"I don't believe you. Tell me how different you are."

"He has his own ranch and trains cutting horses."

"You love horses. Just not the hunters your father favors."

True, but that was a minor point. "He's very established, with many friends and neighbors that he's known for years."

"You'd love to have that type of life. You've always wanted to fit in someplace nice and homey."

"His homey place is in *Texas.*"

"So what's wrong with Texas?"

Gwendolyn felt like shaking Alexi. "He believes I'm this wonderfully organized, terribly efficient person who can do anything."

"You are. Well, almost anything. I've asked you several times to change the weather, and you have yet to obey my request."

"Alexi, would you be serious!"

"Gwendolyn, you are extremely competent and talented. If I haven't told you that often enough, I'm sorry. Why don't you believe both of us?"

"Because Hank has only seen me in crisis mode! We weren't together day in and day out, through the everyday ups and downs. For goodness' sake, I'm not exciting! And he's been a champion rodeo star, with adoring women and admiring men. I'm quiet and rather ordinary.''

''So you don't think you'd stack up, so to speak, with his former girlfriends?''

''Crudely put, but yes.''

''Bull. Next argument.''

She huffed out a breath of exasperation. ''He's so confident. Most of the time I feel like a sniveling coward around him.''

''Now, that's the most ridiculous statement you've made all afternoon. You are extremely capable and have every reason to be confident. I constantly throw you into absurd situations and you always shine.''

''Perhaps I have a certain ability to think well on my feet, but that doesn't mean I can compete with Hank McCauley.''

''Gwendolyn,'' Alexi said, taking her hand and turning completely serious, ''where in the world did you ever get the idea that life…or love, is about competition?''

She sat there in the car as his words washed over her. Competition. When had she learned to think of her relationships that way? When her father compared her to her brother and found her lacking? When she realized she'd never have the flash or glamour of some of her girlfriends? When she discovered she could excel—or ''beat''—others at academic or professional challenges?

''Hank said I can't let my father's approval rule my life.''

''Well, he's absolutely right. I wish I could have been the one to make you see the truth, but I'm glad you finally grasped the idea. You are your own person, Gwendolyn. The only person you ever have to please is yourself. The only person you will ever compete against is yourself.''

She looked at Alexi and finally realized the truth that had been evading her for years. For her entire adult life. She could never be happy by trying to please someone else, especially someone she didn't even agree with. A feeling of relief washed over her, putting tears in her eyes. Through the watery veil, Alexi appeared as Hank, with his deep concern and abundance of caring. She began to cry, not because she'd lost the man she loved, but because she'd finally realized that love didn't respect the boundaries of time or countries.

Alexi didn't say another word, just wrapped her in his arms and held her like the good friend he'd always been.

In a moment, he asked, ''Are you ready to go back to him?''

''Oh, Alexi, if I do, I'll be leaving you in the lurch. I can't—''

''No, you must. I can always hire another public relations coordinator, but you're my best friend.''

His admission made her cry all over again. By the time she stopped, she realized the Land Rover was no longer moving.

''What's wrong?''

''I'm just trying to decide if we should turn around or drop me off first and let Mr. Boedecker take you back to Ranger Springs.'' Alexi leaned forward and asked, ''How far are we from the airport?''

''Maybe another half an hour,'' the driver said.

''Then I think we should continue. I really need to get on the plane before I decide to join Lady Gwendolyn when she runs away.''

"Am I really running away?"

"Yes, you are," he said. "After all these years of putting up with my sudden absences, you get to experience the pure joy of running away. Or, in this case, running toward your destiny."

"I'll miss the challenge of your sudden disappearances," she answered with a sad smile.

"I'll miss you, too, but nothing says you have to stay in Texas all the time. You know where I'll be if you want to visit."

"And you know where I'll be."

His eyes lost their sparkle when he replied, "I believe I'd better stay away from Texas for a while. Perhaps a dozen years or so. Perhaps after I marry the woman my father chooses and produce my own little heirs."

"Oh, Alexi."

"Don't feel sorry for me, Gwendolyn. I've known where my duty rests for years."

But Alexi hadn't know he was going to be the crown prince of Belegovia when he was growing up, and therein lay the problem. "Yes, but—"

"There is no 'but' in the royal palace," Alexi said. He leaned toward the front seat. "Continue on to the airport, Mr. Boedecker. Then take Lady Gwendolyn back to Ranger Springs posthaste."

"I believe," she said with a smile she felt all the way through to her toes, "that you'd best become accustomed to calling me Wendy."

HE HAD A LOT OF WORK backed up, Hank thought as he pulled on an old pair of jeans and boots. He rolled up the sleeves of his worn chambray shirt and tried to think of the new bay gelding he'd gotten in two days ago, the upcoming quarter horse sale, and all his plans for his future.

His efforts were about as futile as recalling the multiplication tables while making love—sometimes a man just had to concentrate on what was important. And right now, the most important person in his life was boarding a plane for Belegovia.

He jammed his hat on his head, pulled the brim low over his eyes and stalked toward the barn. The horses didn't train themselves. They also didn't clean out their own stalls or fill up their feed buckets. Fortunately for him, he had plenty to do since Juan was off on Sunday. Nothing like chores to keep his mind off losing the woman he loved, he thought as he charged through the door of the tack room.

A half an hour later, tired and sweating from working the new horse on the lunge line, he pulled off his hat and wiped his forehead. Hard work in the hot sun hadn't made him forget his Lady Wendy. He wondered how long, how many days, before he could get through five minutes without thinking of her.

He hadn't given up on going to Belegovia to fetch her home…if she didn't come to her senses soon, admit she loved him and come back on her own. If he did have to go get her, she'd be all upset at first, but he was pretty sure that if he could kiss her and call her darlin', she'd be back in his arms for good. Eventually.

He had to convince her they were one-hundred-percent right for each other. He'd have to be better than when he was playing Prince Alexi, because the stakes were a lot higher than the future of some country or the wishes of some king.

He settled his hat back on his head and looked back

at the bay. The horse stared back, his ears flicking back and forth as if he was listening to something. Just as Hank was about to snap the end of the long lunge line, signaling the workout to resume, the sound of a vehicle on the gravel road broke through the silence of the afternoon.

Hank closed his eyes and said a silent prayer that the paparazzi and tabloid journalists hadn't driven out here to harass him. Didn't they have their story? Weren't they convinced he and Kerry had run off for a few days of slap and tickle at the beach?

He wanted to ignore the sound of the gravel crunching, but he couldn't. No telling what those crazy journalists would do while looking for a story. With a sigh he gathered in the lunge line and walked the gelding toward the fence.

He looked through the rails. Whoever was coming was in a black SUV, churning up dust in its wake. He blinked, not sure what he was seeing for a moment. Maybe his mind was playing tricks on him, but it looked like Prince Alexi's Land Rover.

Instead of tying the gelding, he unclipped the lunge line and turned the horse loose inside the pen. With his eyes still focused on the Land Rover, Hank swung open the gate and walked toward the open area between the house and barn.

Damn those dark tinted windows! He couldn't see inside as the SUV came to a stop sideways in the drive. Had the whole group returned? Did they need something else from him?

Pete Boedecker opened the driver's door, then walked around the back and removed a suitcase and overnight case. Hank heard the back door slam as he stood staring at the Land Rover. In just a moment,

Pete walked around the driver's door, flashed him a grin and a thumbs-up sign and got inside. He started the engine, put the SUV in gear and drove away.

Leaving Hank staring at Lady Gwendolyn Reed.

She stood there in that prissy, too-hot wool suit she'd worn to the press conference, her hands clasped in front of her. He couldn't see the expression on her face, but as he strode toward her, he vowed he would. See her, talk to her, touch her.

Then he was taking her inside and not letting her out again until she decided to stay forever.

He stopped in front of her, his heart racing, as he waited for her to explain why she was here.

She tilted her chin up and said, "You never did tell me what your fee was for pretending to be the prince. Other than that one night on the Riverwalk, which I believe was partial payment."

"So you're here to settle up?"

"Yes."

"All by yourself?"

"Yes," she answered, looking a little nervous. "Prince Alexi is already on his jet, probably in the air right now."

Hank stepped closer until they were toe to toe. "I don't suppose you brought the Belegovian treasury with you."

"No, I didn't."

"Then, darlin', there's only one way I can get paid for my time."

"And what is that?"

He picked her up in his arms. "My fee for impersonatin' the prince, for putting up with all that fussin', for lyin' to the press and my friends, is you."

"Me?"

"Yes." He narrowed his eyes and frowned. "For someone who usually has a lot to say, you're awfully quiet. Are you gonna answer in one-syllable words forever?"

"No," she said, grinning as she looped her arms around his neck.

Hank nodded toward the luggage. "Do you have anything in there with red lace, cut low at the top and high at the bottom?"

"No, I don't. Why?"

"I'm just tryin' to decide if there's any reason I should carry your luggage into the house before I make love to you."

Wendy laughed, then her expression sobered. "You were right, Hank. Alexi made me realize several things about myself, but mostly he made me believe that what I was feeling was real. I was afraid to trust my heart." She paused, her whiskey eyes serious as she gazed at him. "I love you, Hank."

He kissed her, then whispered against her lips. "I love you, too, darlin'."

"And I love your ranch. I don't want to be anywhere else on earth but right here, with you."

"Good, because I was tryin' to be real patient. I'd probably have given you until next week to come to your senses. Then I would have flown over there and brought you back home."

"Home," she said, looking around with misty eyes. "I like the sound of that."

"Good, because I can't just up and move. There's not a real big market for cuttin' horses in England."

"And where would we ever find an aquifer-fed pool, or a Texas sunset? Or go walking along the river like in San Antonio?"

"Heck, darlin', I haven't even shown you most of the state. We're barely gettin' to the good parts."

"How long do you think that will take?" she asked, running her cool hand down the side of his face.

"About fifty or sixty years."

She leaned close and whispered against his lips, "Perfect."

He kissed her in the middle of his yard, with the Texas sun beating down on them and the smells of approaching summer drifting through the hills. And then he carried her inside the house, her luggage forgotten as he made love to her...and made her the lady of his heart forever.

Just what *happened between Kerry Lynn
and Prince Alexi during
their few days together?
Read their story next month in the
concluding book of
Victoria Chancellor's series*

A ROYAL TWIST
THE PRINCE'S TEXAS BRIDE HAR #959

Turn the page for a sneak peek!

Prologue

Kerry Lynn Jacks pulled her blue chenille robe tight around her, fought down another urge to run into the bathroom and headed instead for the insistent pounding on her door. This had better be important. Mornings were *not* her best time of day. Hadn't been ever since that little test strip had turned blue—and she'd started turning green.

She wove her way around her coffee table and chair. The tile in the entryway to her apartment was cool on her bare feet even though August in Texas was anything but temperate. "This had better not be someone selling magazine subscriptions," she murmured to herself as she stood on tiptoe and peered through the peephole.

Her heart began to pound and she sucked in a much-needed breath. Either her friend Hank McCauley had started wearing designer clothing or there was a prince on her doorstep. Either way, she had to let him in.

She turned the dead bolt and doorknob, then took a shaky step back as the door swung open.

The man standing before her looked intense and extremely sexy as he glared at her from beneath furrowed brows.

Definitely the prince.

"Hello, Alexi," she said hoarsely, past the lump in her throat that she couldn't attribute to morning sickness.

"Why didn't you tell me?"

She couldn't pretend not to know what he was talking about. "I was going to." She shrugged, then crossed her arms over her chest. "I just hadn't decided how or when. You're not exactly the easiest person in the world to get in touch with."

"It's been three months!"

"Well, yes, but it's only been about a month and a half since I was sure."

He ran a hand through his hair, looking suddenly weary. "Can we go inside and talk about this?"

"Of course." She stepped back and gestured toward the living room. "Make yourself comfortable."

She followed him, adjusting her robe, smoothing her blond hair into some semblance of order. The very feminine part of her wished she looked better—more pulled together, with a bit of makeup to hid behind. But Alexi would probably see through whatever cosmetics she might apply, so why bother? And since she'd already decided to tell him the truth, what did she have to hide…except her pride?

"If you want some coffee, you'll have to make it. My stomach…well, let's just say I've given up on my morning jolt of caffeine for a while." She sank into the chair across from the couch and curled her feet beneath her.

"I didn't travel thousands of miles for coffee, even though I'm sure yours is excellent."

"I've had a lot of experience making coffee," she commented casually, reminding Prince Alexi Ladislas of Belegovia that she had been a lowly truck-stop waitress when they'd met. Reminding him that they lived in separate worlds and always would.

"Dammit, Kerry, you should have phoned me immediately."

"And what could you have done if you'd known a month or two ago? I'm having this baby whether you know about it or not."

"Then you admit it? This is my child?"

"This is *my* child," she stated, placing her hand over her slightly rounded stomach. "Maybe conception was an accident, but I want this baby. I don't need permission from you or anyone else to deliver my son or daughter."

"You think I don't want you to have the baby? Don't be absurd. I would never—"

"I thought I did at one time, but now I realize I don't know you well enough to know how you would react. We didn't have much time to discuss the subject in the short time we spent together."

He leaned forward and placed his forearms on his knees. "We managed to talk about almost everything else."

Kerry bowed her head and took a deep breath. She would not cry in front of him, even though her nerves were as jumbled as her thoughts. Even though her stomach constricted with tension and she had the urge to run out of the room.

"I suppose you found out from Gwendolyn." The idea that her friend had called him and revealed a confidence sickened her. Kerry thought she was a good judge of people, and Gwendolyn had seemed like such a loyal friend. But she'd been Alexi's childhood buddy and then a trusted employee for years. Maybe that went beyond a three-month friendship based mostly on a set of bizarre circumstances that few people would believe...and even fewer knew to be true.

"She didn't call me to reveal your secret, if that's what you're thinking," Alexi said. "I was actually on the phone to her when you came to the ranch."

Kerry frowned, remembering yesterday's conversation clearly. "She told me she had to put a call on hold."

"Gwendolyn has many good qualities and abilities, but anything above the technology of a manual pencil sharpener is beyond her. She obviously didn't put me on hold because I heard every word. I immediately flew to Texas and went to your house so we could resolve the problem, but your mother informed me that you were living in your own apartment."

"My baby is not a problem!"

"I didn't mean it that way," he said quickly. "I meant that I wanted to talk to you about the situation." He looked up. "At least your mother was glad to see me."

"I'll bet. She had your autograph framed, you know." Charlene Jacks had probably loved playing matchmaker. It's a wonder she hadn't phoned to tell Kerry that a prince was on his way to her apartment. Of course, her mother didn't yet know *why* Prince Alexi might be in such a snit. And if he'd asked her to remain silent so he could surprise Kerry with his mere presence, she would have complied in a heartbeat.

"Why did you tell Gwendolyn instead of calling me?"

"I was so upset. I didn't know who else to talk to. I didn't even tell my mother, for Pete's sake!"

Kerry took another deep breath, wishing she had some soda crackers and ginger ale to calm her queasiness. She wouldn't go into the kitchen to get them when she and Alexi were in the middle of this conversation. Even though she didn't want to discuss her baby at this moment, she knew she'd have to face him sooner or later.

"I just needed advice," she admitted in a small voice. She looked into his eyes and saw a fading of anger. A smidgen of sympathy. "I needed to determine what I should do that would be the most fair to everyone. You, me and the baby."

"And she told you about Belegovia's laws of succession."

"Yes." She'd been surprised when Gwendolyn had volunteered the information, but then Kerry had realized that she had to consider all these factors to decide what was best for her baby.

"So you know that whether you have a boy or a girl, this child could succeed me as king or queen."

"Yes," Kerry said, lifting her chin, "but only if you declare it as your heir. Otherwise, any children you and—" she choked out the words "—the contessa have after your marriage will be your legitimate heirs. This baby would still be the half sibling of the royal heirs, but wouldn't be in line for the throne."

Alexi leaned forward, his expression once again fierce. "First of all, I'm not marrying Contessa di Giovanni."

"But my mother told me that there was a big party this weekend where your engagement was going to be announced." Charlene Jacks was an avid royal watcher and had kept Kerry informed of every event involving Belegovia—until she'd realized her daughter was hopelessly in love with the prince.

Alexi held up his hand, obviously impatient. "Second, there won't be any half siblings."

She knew that as the crown prince, he'd be expected to have at least two children to ensure the succession. His father, King Wilheim, had given him an ultimatum of age thirty to find a bride. Which had led him to run away while on a trip to Texas in May.

He'd run away with *her*.

Kerry's stomach tightened as she asked, "Why?"

He covered her hands with his, making her look into his sky-blue eyes. Her heart pounded at the warmth and strength of his grasp, the scent of his cologne. She hadn't seen him for three months, but it seemed like only three days.

When he spoke, his voice was softer, more intimate. "Because you and I are getting married as soon as I can arrange for the ceremony at the cathedral in Belegovia. Our child will be the undisputed *legitimate* heir to the throne."

Kerry took one look at his intense expression and knew it was too late for soda crackers and ginger ale. She leapt from the chair and fled to the bathroom, remembering in vivid detail just exactly how she'd gotten herself pregnant by the prince....